AFTERMATH

AFTERMATH

Peter Turnbull

This first world edition published 2010
in Great Britain and in 2011 in the USA by
SEVERN HOUSE PUBLISHERS LTD of
9–15 High Street, Sutton, Surrey, England, SM1 1DF.
Trade paperback edition first published
in Great Britain and the USA 2011 by
SEVERN HOUSE PUBLISHERS LTD.

British Library Cataloguing in Publication Data

Turnbull, Peter, 1950–
     Aftermath. – (The Hennessey and Yellich series)
     1. Hennessey, George (Fictitious character) – Fiction.
     2. Yellich, Somerled (Fictitious character) – Fiction.
     3. Police – England – Yorkshire – Fiction. 4. Serial murder
     investigation – Fiction. 5. Detective and mystery stories.
     I. Title II. Series
     823.9'14-dc22

ISBN-13: 978-0-7278-6969-2   (cased)
ISBN-13: 978-1-84751-299-4   (trade paper)

All Severn House titles are printed on acid-free paper.

Severn House Publishers support The Forest Stewardship Council [FSC],
the leading international forest certification organisation. All our titles that
are printed on Greenpeace-approved FSC-certified paper carry the FSC logo.

Mixed Sources
Product group from well-managed
forests and other controlled sources
www.fsc.org Cert no. SA-COC-1565
© 1996 Forest Stewardship Council
FSC

Typeset by Palimpsest Book Production Ltd.,
Falkirk, Stirlingshire.
Printed and bound in Great Britain by the
MPG Books Group, Bodmin, Cornwall.

PROLOGUE

'It's the look, that short-lived look in their eyes.' The man smiled at the recollection of pleasant memories.

'When they realize what's happening . . . that look of betrayal. I mean that they realize that they have been betrayed.' The woman hooked her arm inside the man's arm as they walked.

'It's always the same,' the man replied, 'like will find like. You found me and I found you.'

'Like finds like,' the woman echoed.

They halted to enjoy the view across the Vale of York to where the City of York lay nestled amid a lush patchwork of fields and small stands of woodland.

'It's like an addict with his drug . . . you need the next fix . . . you need the next look in the victim's eyes.'

'And you need a partner you can trust,' the woman added. 'It's all about trust.'

'Yes . . . I knew we were made for each other . . . I saw it in your eyes.'

The woman laughed softly. 'The cat was the first . . . that old cat . . . years ago now.'

'Yes, but the look that flashed across its eyes was identical.'

'Delicious . . . delicious. And we were both still at school then.'

'No. I had already left . . . one year ahead of you. Remember? But all so naive and needy.'

'All so naive or so needy, mainly needy . . . but all had that same look in the eyes when their time came.'

'A few escaped,' the woman commented as her eye was drawn to a hovering sparrowhawk above the adjacent field.

'What was that girl's name . . .? Tilly something . . . she didn't keep the rendezvous . . . saved her life by doing so . . . it was like she smelled a rat. She didn't report us though.'

'She had nothing to report. We just invited her to go to the coast with us.'

'We should have kept photographs.' The woman sighed.

'That would have been suicidal. They have nothing to link us to them when they are found and I want to continue to enjoy walks like this, on days like this, for a few years yet.'

'I suppose you are right . . . glad we stopped though . . . you were right about that. Quit while ahead . . . but those looks they gave at the end . . . those looks . . . heavenly.'

ONE

Wednesday, 10th June – 10.05 hours to 16.35 hours
in which an enclosed garden gives up its dead.

John Seers tried to analyse his fear, or his fears. He sat and wondered why it was that he should feel so apprehensive when there was nothing tangible to fear – nothing at all. The large old house was quiet, utterly silent, which was only to be expected because he was the sole person in the building. John Seers reasoned that any other person who might be in the building would probably be just as wary of him as he would be of them. Unless it was not another person in the building but other persons, then, then he would have cause to fear. But he was alone, he was quite definitely the only human being in the house, and not only was he alone but people knew where he was and would come looking for him should he fall and fracture his leg or sustain some other disabling mishap, and thus not return by the appointed hour. He also carried his mobile phone, and even though the old house was remote, the signal strength had proved quite adequate should he need to summon assistance. In the end John Seers concluded that he was fearing only fear itself and that he was experiencing the sense of vulnerability, quite intensely so, of being a lone human being. Human beings, Seers reasoned, have achieved dominance because they have developed technology and because they function in cooperating groups, but as individuals, without technology, shelter, or a means to start a life saving and/or defensive fire, then the human being is vulnerable and an easy prey for many predators. Seers was content in the knowledge that he was alone in the house, and he did not expect to be attacked by a pack of ravenous baboons, nor by a pride of equally hungry lions, but yet, when his eyes fell on an axe helve which lay propped against the scullery wall, cobwebbed and dust covered, he picked it up and held it in his right hand, comforted by its weight, as he advanced from room to room.

He had decided that the best way to commence the project, which he had been advised would take him some four to six weeks to complete, would be to familiarize himself with the interior of the house, including, of course, the cellar and the attic, and then to visit the outbuildings and finally the overgrown garden. He felt he needed to set foot in all parts of the property and so he walked, wearing summer shoes and lightweight all white coveralls, axe helve in one hand and battery operated torch in the other. He opened each door that he came to and shone the beam of the torch into the rooms from which sunlight had been excluded by heavy curtains drawn shut. The torch beam illuminated strange shapes and shadows and mounds and peaks and valleys of darkness caused by the items in the room being covered by dust sheets. Seers went first into each and every room on the ground floor of the house, penetrating the rooms as much as he found possible, taking his time – not a rapid putting his head round the door of each room, glancing once at the interior and then closing the door behind him before moving on to the next room, but rather he loitered in each room, looking up at the ceiling and down at the floor covering. He marvelled at the good fortune of the house being so remote, so isolated, and so thoroughly concealed from view. A more open location and nearer the city, he fancied, would have led to the house and its contents being plundered by thieves in the night, loading up their white vans and selling the items at Bermondsey antique market. Then would have come the squatters or the local teenagers with stones and bricks, ensuring that not one pane of glass remained intact. Finally would come one or two children, boy children, who did not fully understand what they were doing, or an adult, sinister, lone-acting, who did fully understand what he was doing, but either carrying a can of petrol and a box of matches, and that would have been the fate of Bromyards; all contents purloined, then squatted, then vandalized and finally razed by fire. An unfortunate end to the house initially built in 1719 and added to over the following two hundred and fifty years. Throughout its history it had always been in the hands of the same family, until the last of the line had eventually succumbed to his frailty and failing health, expiring with nearly three hundred years of inheritance around him.

John Seers ascended the wide wooden stairway, which creaked occasionally under his weight, and so he felt obliged to move to the edge of the stairway where he reasoned the structure would have retained more strength, and did so, choosing the banister side because it offered a handhold in the event of a rotten stair giving way. On the upper floor he discovered more rooms, all of which had been used as bedchambers and the contents therein had similarly been covered in dust sheets. The air in the house was stale, the building poorly ventilated and John Seers had difficulty obtaining deep breaths. Nonetheless, he continued to explore the house, becoming increasingly grateful for the person or persons unknown who had draped the contents of the house with dust sheets: it was going to make his job much cleaner. It was on the upper floor that he found the living quarters of the final occupant of Bromyards, and upon finding them felt the poignancy of the man's last years of life. It seemed clear, that, as the years took their toll, the last owner had retreated first from the grounds, then from the garden, then from the house, until his accommodation was just one self-contained room, and a small room at that, with just a single bed of unwashed sheets and a stack of food in tin cans and a two-ringed gas stove to cook on. A toilet directly across the corridor also

doubled as washing facilities for him and any plates and
pans he used when preparing and eating his food. That was
home for him. Not for him was the vastness of Bromyards
and its incalculable cubic feet of volume within its walls and
under its roof, but one small room, which was smaller
and ruder than had been John Seers' accommodation when
he was at university. He closed the door of the small room
with a certain yet distinct reverence.

The attic of Bromyards he found to be as he had expected
it to be; a disorganized receptacle for assorted items not
required in the living area of the house and which were
sufficiently small to be able to be lifted through the trap
door, being its sole point of ingress and egress. He saw also
that a lot of detritus had accumulated since 1719. The
detritus in the attic had not, he noticed with a groan of
dismay, been covered with dust sheets. He dare not proceed
further into the cobwebs and the dust without extra thick
coveralls. He also saw that he would need a base upon
which to stand, there being no proper flooring in the attic,
just beams going across the width of the house with thin
plaster, which would not take his weight between them.
That, though, he reasoned, is what recces are all about. It
is the purpose of a recce, to determine what is where and
also what is going to be needed. He carefully descended
from the attic and returned to the ground floor of the house
and searched and found the entrance to the cellar. In the
cellar he, for some reason, felt particularly vulnerable. As
he swept the room with the beam of his torch he saw that
the contents of the cellar seemed to be similar to that of
the attic, unwanted items which were perhaps larger and
heavier than the ones which had been lifted into the attic.
The cellar, accessed by a flight of stone steps, had been
built in a pattern of ten chambers and had an earthen floor,
which Seers felt was highly unusual for the Vale of York
and its low-lying nature, which rendered it prone to flooding.
Bromyards, he assumed, must occupy an island of high

ground which thusly permitted the excavation of a cellar over which the house was then built.

John Seers emerged from the cellar and left the house by the large front door and began his exploration of the garden and the grounds beyond. Outside he felt uncomfortably warm in his coveralls and kept his eyes downcast to shield them from the glare of the sun, which by mid forenoon was already high in the sky. He found he felt safer in the garden and so reasoned that the fear he had experienced in the house must have been generated by the gloom and the restricted vision of seeing nothing beyond whichever room or corridor he was in at any one time, and yet knowing he was within a very large and unoccupied house. Yet, once in the garden he could survey a greater area illuminated by sunlight and so would have earlier warning of the approach of any threat. Despite this, he still felt comforted and reassured by the axe helve he continued to hold.

He probed his way through the grass which had grown to waist height in places and heard the scurrying of rodents within the grass as they timidly ran at his approach. The grounds were massively overgrown with grasses dominating the vegetation. Although Seers was able to make out parts of the garden, the border of a lawn, the row of oak trees, the apple orchard with the boughs sagging under the great weight of fruit, he could not exactly say where the garden had ended and the wilderness of the grounds began.

Remaining near the house, he found that the outbuildings were of a solid wooden construction and it seemed, like the house, that they appeared to be still in a structurally sound condition. They had clearly been very well maintained and it looked as if the last person to have had responsibility for them had applied a generous seal of weatherproofing to the buildings in anticipation of them being abandoned. Within the buildings were garden tools of an earlier era, solid and heavy and still functional, although an ancient lawnmower had become badly corroded and Seers guessed it was worth only scrap value. The garage amid the buildings contained a Talbot of 1930s' vintage which had been left resting on wooden blocks so as to preserve the suspension as much as possible, and when Seers opened the driver's door he found that the interior of the car smelled richly of leather and he experienced a they-don't-make-'em-like-this-anymore moment. Seers knew little about cars but he sensed that the Talbot could be restored and that it was an item of high value. Leaving the garage, he waded through waist-high grass to a gazebo, the paint of which had peeled over many summers. He ventured towards the structure and found that it seemed solid and immovable. Clearly it had settled and set upon the mechanism on which it had once been rotated in accordance with the movement of the sun across the sky. Unlike the other outbuildings, the gazebo would, so Seers thought, be earmarked for demolition. Brushing a persistent fly from his face Seers turned to the kitchen garden. It was the only part of the property mentioned in the schedule that he had not yet visited. He thought a glance at the kitchen garden and then the overview of Bromyards would be complete and thus a good morning's work be achieved. He would lunch in the village and then return to commence work proper that afternoon.

The kitchen garden was, he discovered, an area of approximately one hundred yards by fifty yards, and was bordered, or enclosed, by a brick wall of some ten feet in height and which had been painted white, as he was to find, on both the interior and the exterior surfaces, with the topmost line of bricks painted black. As had only to be expected, the paint had faded and peeled on the south-facing walls and on the topmost bricks. Access to the kitchen garden was by a single green painted wooden door set, curiously Seers thought, in the section of the wall which was furthest from the house, needlessly extending the walk between the kitchen garden to the kitchen itself. He followed the overgrown path, which led from the house to the kitchen garden with the northern facing wall of the garden to his right. He turned at the end of the wall and stood in front of the door. To his dismay he saw that the door was lockable and he envisaged having to break down the door, leaving the new owners, whoever they may be, to build a replacement.

The door, in the event, had not been locked and the key then placed on one side, unlabelled. To Seer's surprise it not only opened but it swung open easily, moving silently on its hinges, and at that instant John Seers was stabbed with a sense of real fear, not the fear of the unknown that he had felt in the house, not the fearing of fear itself, not the fear which had largely evaporated upon his leaving the house and stepping out of doors into the sun-drenched garden, but this was fear created by observation, and by logical deduction caused by common sense, or what his cloth-cap wearing coal-mining grandfather would have called 'gumption'. Unlike all the other doors in Bromyards, except for the bedroom of the last occupant, which protested when opened because their hinges had seized from under use, the door of the kitchen garden opened noiselessly on lubricated hinges. 'Gumption' told him that the door had been frequently and recently used. As the old man had been lying dying in a small room in his huge house, someone, or some persons had been accessing the kitchen garden for purpose or purposes unknown, although the lubricated hinges were testament to the fact that he or she, or they, wished their activity to remain undetected. A house full of valuables, and so easily removed, yet someone was interested only in the kitchen garden? John Seers knew fear and, cautiously, he pushed the door open.

He did not notice the bodies at first. The first thing he saw was the ivy clad surfaces of the walls. Also ivy covered was a large greenhouse still with, so far as he could tell, all panes of glass still intact. All the hinged panes were closed and Seers knew that that would make the interior of the greenhouse insufferably hot within, he would have to open the windows to allow the structure to 'breathe' and then return some time later. The remainder of the kitchen garden was extensively overgrown and once again grasses had come to dominate the vegetable patches. It was when he once again noticed how aggressive grass becomes when an area of land is left unattended that the skull grinned at him. He stood, startled for an instant, and then he felt that the skull, human, bleached by the sun and inclined in his direction was not grinning but was somehow saying, 'Help me, help me', and beyond the first skull was a second, also human, and beyond that a third. John Seers did not look any further but turned, slowly, and walked back to what he felt to be the safety of his car, and there he took his mobile from his pocket and pressed three nines and told the officer what he had found. 'Directions?' he replied to the next query. 'Oh, you'll never find it,' he glanced at the road map he had followed earlier that morning, 'drive on the road between Leavening and Thixendale . . . don't know its number, it's not given on this map. I'll wait on the road and make myself known to the attending officer. Tell him to look for a bloke in white coveralls standing by a red Vauxhall.'

George Hennessey slowed as he approached the police patrol car, and as he did so the officer standing beside the vehicle drew himself up and stiffened into a near 'at attention' position and pointed to the driveway that was the approach to Bromyards. Hennessey turned into the driveway and nodded in response to the officer's salute. The driveway, Hennessey found, was long, probably a mile he guessed from the road to the house, and was being severely encroached upon by the vegetation at either side, so much so that he felt he was driving his car down a narrow tunnel of endless shrubbery. At the top, or the end of the driveway, the foliage gave way to an open gravel-covered courtyard within which police vehicles, a red Vauxhall, and two black, windowless mortuary department vans were parked. Also in the courtyard was a second unmarked car and a van belonging to the Scene of Crime Unit. Hennessey parked his car beside the mortuary vans and scowled at the drivers and drivers' assistants of the vans who stood irreverently smoking cigarettes, and were chatting idly, commenting it seemed on articles printed in the day's tabloid press. One of the men responded to Hennessey's scowl by flicking his cigarette defiantly on to the ground and crushing it beneath his foot, all the while holding eye contact with Hennessey. Hennessey, not having any authority over the mortuary van crewmen, could only look away from them as he got out of his car, putting his jacket and panama hat on as he did so. He enquired of a white-shirted constable the whereabouts of DC Webster and, following the constable's directions, walked slowly but with quiet confidence to the kitchen garden wherein he found Webster talking to a scene of crime officer, and as he approached he thought that both men appeared distinctly shaken. Webster smiled briefly at Hennessey as Hennessey approached him.

'Thank you for coming so quickly, sir.' Webster spoke quietly, calmly. 'This is bad. It's big and bad and one for you, sir.'

'What do we have?'

'So far . . . so far we have five skeletons. Seem to my untrained eye to be exhibiting different rates of decomposition. One is completely skeletal; one still has tissue in evidence.'

'Five?' Hennessey raised an eyebrow. 'So far?'

'Yes, sir, so far.' Webster glanced at the garden where three white-shirted constables were carefully probing the vegetation. 'As you see, sir, the garden is badly overgrown . . . a few more skeletons, or corpses may still be concealed but we're moving carefully . . . don't want to damage the evidence.'

'Yes . . . a large area search. You don't need more men?'

'I think not, sir.' Webster brushed a fly from his face. 'Many hands might well make light work but in this case I think it is more true that too many cooks will spoil the broth.'

'I see.'

'It's also the apparent case that all the bodies are local-ized within this area . . . within these walls, eventually we'll locate them and do so quite rapidly.'

'So in this . . . remnant of the kitchen garden? Not within the house or the grounds?'

'They'll be searched, of course, sir, but the gentleman who found them mentioned that the hinges of the garden door have been lubricated, uniquely in the house and grounds.'

'I see,' Hennessey watched a constable part the branches of a laurel bush, 'that is a fair point.' He turned again to Webster. 'You look shaken, Webster. It's not like you.'

'I am, sir. It's not just the skeletons; it's the way that they were restrained.'

'They were restrained?'

'Yes, sir . . . wrists chained together behind their backs and one of their ankles was attached to a long, heavy chain which ran the length of the garden, anchored certainly at this end in a block of concrete. They also seem to have remnants of some type of gag in their mouths.'

'A gag,' Hennessey gasped, 'so suggesting they were alive when left here . . . attached to a chain . . .?'

'Yes, sir . . . in full view of the previous skeletons . . . and left to succumb to thirst or cold. If left in the summer thirst would have taken them, if in winter hypothermia.'

'Better show me.' Hennessey followed Webster who led him to the skeleton which was closest to the door of the garden. 'I've asked the pathologist to attend, sir,' Webster explained, 'no need for the police surgeon to confirm life extinct in the matter of corpses, as per regulations.'

'Yes . . . good.'

'This is what I mean, sir.' Webster stood over the skeleton of the human being. 'The SOCO have taken all photographs.'

Hennessey looked at the corpse and as he did so, he noticed a silence about the scene, even the birds were silent. Hennessey saw instantly that the scene was exactly as Webster had described. The skeleton lay on its side with what appeared to be a length of rope fastened in its mouth tied behind the neck. The rope had largely rotted to the point of disintegration but it was a clear illustration of a simple but efficient gag. It was all that was needed to prevent the victim screaming or shouting for assistance. The wrists, as Webster had further indicated, were fastened closely together by a small length of lightweight chain and fastened with two small brass padlocks, and the left ankle had been fastened with a similar length of lightweight chain to a long length of heavy chain. The heavy chain would, by itself, be difficult to pull or drag along the ground but it was, as Webster had indicated, buried at one end and doubtless at the other end also, into large blocks of concrete. 'Premeditated,' he said.

'Sir?'

'The way the chain is embedded into the concrete . . . it seems that the chain was covered with concrete powder when it was in a large plastic bucket and the concrete moistened and allowed to harden, but that amount of concrete would take weeks to harden . . . or "cure" as I believe is the correct term.'

'I see what you mean, sir, and it would seem like that was done here . . .'

'Yes, that's what I was thinking. It would be much easier to transport two plastic buckets, some bags of cement, a length of chain and an amount of water and assemble the thing here . . . bring a little at a time and take a few days over the operation. That is premeditation.'

'It is, isn't it, sir?' Webster looked at the length of chain to where it disappeared into undergrowth, by then being probed by the three constables. 'So the chain and the blocks of concrete were in place before the first victim was brought here?'

'It seems likely . . . and the skeletons are of different ages, you say?' Hennessey considered the crime scene.

'It appears so, sir. As you see it's badly run down. The owner . . . the last owner . . . died recently.'

'I see. Well, dead or not he is going to be our number one suspect.'

'It would seem likely, sir, but frankly I doubt that will be the case, not after what Mr Seers told me.'

'Mr Seers? Who is he?'

'The member of the public who found the skeletons . . . he saw three . . . and raised the alarm. We subsequently discovered two further skeletons and at which point you arrived, sir.'

'Very well,' Hennessey brushed another fly away from his face. 'Is he still here?'

'Yes, sir, he is the owner of the red Vauxhall parked in front of the house.'

'Yes, I noticed it. I'll go and talk to him. If you would carry on here, please?'

'Yes, sir.'

George Hennessey walked slowly from the kitchen garden to the front of the house where the motor vehicles were parked and where, as the day had matured, some element of shade was by then afforded. He identified the red Vauxhall and approached it calmly, smiling gently at the composed looking man who sat in the driver's seat. 'Mr Seers?'

'Yes, that's me,' Seers opened the car door and stepped out of the vehicle, 'John Seers of Seers, Seers and Noble.'

'A solicitor?'

'Yes, for my sins,' Seers shrugged, 'but it pays the bills.'

'I haven't heard of your firm, I regret to say.'

'We hardly do any criminal work which probably

explains it . . . not a great deal of money to be made defending murderers. Our firm is principally concerned with commercial law and property . . . if the property is large and valuable enough.'

Hennessey indicated Bromyards, 'This sort of large and valuable?'

'Yes, this sort of large and valuable. This particular case is quite rare and I pulled rank to get it . . . I am a senior partner . . . it's a job that we could give to a junior but I really wanted it, seemed it was going to get me out of our office for a few weeks.'

'I can understand that,' Hennessey agreed, 'I too dislike being desk-bound. So what exactly were you . . . your firm . . . engaged to do in respect of this property?'

'To make an inventory of the contents.' Seers was tall, clean-shaven, a thin but balanced face. He spoke with received pronunciation so George Hennessey noticed and heard. 'We act for the deceased and the family of the deceased, being one Nicholas Housecarl by name. He was a long-time client of our firm and he left a will in which he directed that his entire estate be liquidated . . . everything, Bromyards and its contents, his portfolio of stocks and shares . . . everything to be turned into cash and then said cash to be distributed in set percentages of the whole to surviving relatives and designated charities.'

'I see,' Hennessey paused. 'Is Bromyards the full name of the property, not House, Hall, Court, Manor . . . or any such name?'

'No other or second name. The house is called simply "Bromyards".'

'I see.'

'So the first step and the one which would have got me out of our office for quite a few weeks was to make an inventory of the contents.'

'No small task.'

'No small task at all, especially when one considers that

the items within the house have been accumulating since 1719.'

'Which is when the house was built?'

'Which is when the house was built, at the beginning of the reign of George I and in the era of Handel and Bach, and . . . I glanced at my son's history books before I began the inventory . . . just to make it even more interesting,' Seers explained with a brief smile. 'I really don't carry that sort of historical knowledge in my head.'

'Impressed, nonetheless.'

'Well, I have to detail everything inside the house . . . and I mean everything . . . from the recently purchased twenty-first century tea mugs in the living area to the dust-sheet covered paintings, which may be old masters lost to the world for centuries and may be worth more than the house itself . . . all has to be catalogued. A very, very interesting job.'

'Sounds so, and I can understand why you pulled rank to get it.'

'Indeed . . . then we have to take the contents into storage by a firm of reputable auctioneers and valued. We use Myles and Innche.'

'Miles and Inch,' Hennessey grinned.

'Yes, it is an unusual name . . . both units of linear measurement . . . but not spelled the same.' Seers told Hennessey how the auctioneers was correctly spelled.

'All right . . . so the owner . . . the last owner died recently?'

'Very recently . . . a matter of days ago. Poor old gentleman, you see, he had all this to live in . . . all this garden and the grounds beyond the garden . . . all of it was his and yet his final days were spent in a little room where he cooked, ate and slept, and he used a bathroom across the corridor for his ablutions. He lived in something akin to a dole collector's miserable accommodation . . . and just look at the state of the gardens. Mr Housecarl was a career soldier and his last action in life was a systematic retreat, first from the garden and then from the house, little by little, until he had just one room and a bathroom upstairs on the first floor, and there he made his last stand, fortunately for me, covering the contents of each room with dust sheets before closing the door of said room behind him for the final time.'

'Eventually fetching up in a box room on the first floor?'

'So it would seem.'

'He would normally be our number one suspect, but it seems that he might have known nothing of what was going on outside his house.'

'Yes . . . as I pointed out to the other officers . . . the doors, you see . . . apart from the door of his box room and the bathroom he used, apart from those two doors, all the hinges on all the doors had stiffened with long-term non-use.'

'Hasn't been opened in years, you mean?'

'If you like, yes, had not been opened in years. That is also apart from the back door and the door of the porch which enclosed it. He had a service from the Meals on Wheels people or rather a privately owned catering company. Meals on Wheels proper provides a service only to those folk who live below a certain income level.'

'Yes . . . yes.'

'And I understand that a district nurse called once or twice a week, so he was probably visited about four days out of seven.'

'I see . . . that is useful to know, thanks.'

'So, just four doors opened with ease.'

'Back porch, back door, his bedroom door and his bath-room door?'

'Yes. All the others were stiff, seized with, as you say, not being opened in years but . . . but . . . the door to the kitchen garden had been lubricated. It just did not open easily, it opened almost silently.'

'Almost silently?'

'Yes, as though it was overdue for lubrication. I knew then that something was amiss . . . but I didn't think . . . wow . . .' Seers shook his head slowly, 'three skeletons . . . all in a row.'

Hennessey kept his own counsel in respect of the discovery of two further skeletons. 'How long had the deceased, your client, been housebound?'

'I don't know, but from my examination of the house I think it could have been a very long time . . . twenty, twenty-five years.'

'As long as that?'

'Well, he was ninety-seven when he expired, so probably in his seventies when he became housebound. The meals delivery people and the medical people will be able to help you there.'

'Yes, we'll be talking to them.'

'The kitchen garden could have been abandoned thirty plus years ago . . . the outbuildings . . . it was like going back in time, a car from the 1930s, a lawnmower of similar age, really robust looking garden tools, the sort of kit that would last a gardener all his working life.' Seers paused. 'Sorry, this is your area of expertise, not mine, but some years ago, long time ago now, when my wife and I were newly married and in our first house . . . our next door neighbour was an elderly lady . . . lovely old soul and we noticed how she was often, and I mean very frequently, visited by youths and children, even as young as twelve years, girls as well as boys. She used to call them her "young visitors". Said young visitors always carried bags which appeared to be laden when they arrived and empty when they left just a few moments later, so they were not stealing from her house and because of that we delayed calling the police . . . you gentlemen . . . but we did eventually phone the police.'

'They were depositing stolen goods in her house to collect later.'

'Yes,' Seers nodded, 'that was it exactly.'

'I was ahead of you . . . that does happen from time to time, sadly so,' Hennessey growled, 'makes you angry.'

'Yes,' Seers glanced at the sky and mopped his brow, 'it made us very angry . . . all the people in the area, not just my wife and I. Lovely old lady and they were exploiting her like that. I mention that incident because the same thing probably happened here . . . someone . . . some felons chanced upon Bromyards and realized that it provided an excellent place to deposit illegal matter. Not stolen goods, as in the case of the elderly lady's house all those years ago . . . but bodies. I mean, three skeletons all in a row . . . even I know that that has to be murder.'

'Indeed . . .' Hennessey replied and at that moment his attention was drawn to a red and white Riley circa 1947, which was driven slowly and was carefully parked beside a police patrol car. As he watched the car Hennessey felt a rush of warmth within him and his chest seemed to expand.

'Lovely old car,' Seers commented. 'It looks quite at home here.'

'Yes, it belongs to our pathologist. I'll have to go and talk to her . . . but thank you, Mr Seers, it's been very useful. One of my colleagues will have to call on you and take a written statement in the next few days.'

'Of course,' Seers smiled. 'I quite expect that.'

'But thank you again.'

Strange things had happened to the man during his life, strange other-worldly supernatural experiences, such as the elderly relative who appeared to him at what transpired to be the precise moment of her death and who looked at him with warning and admonition and disapproval in her eyes. He had also once walked into an alley in a northern city and sensed that 'something happened' in the alley, and later found out that a violent murder had once occurred there.

The ghosts he had seen, three all told, in his life, when other people in his company saw nothing of them. He also knew that things had happened before any news was broken or any report made. He was sitting in the front room of his home reading the *Yorkshire Post* when he put the paper down and stood and walked into the kitchen, where his slender wife was preparing their lunch, and said, 'They've been found.'

His wife turned and nodded solemnly, and replied, 'I know,' she sliced potatoes and dropped them into the steamer, 'this morning.'

'You said nothing?'

'I was waiting to see if you felt it. If you hadn't said anything I would have told you after lunch.'

'I see. When did it come to you?'

'About fifteen minutes ago.'

'They will be finding them just now in that case.'

'Yes,' his wife replied calmly. 'So now we have to wait; now we will find out if we were as careful as we thought we were.'

'We took all the top clothes to charity shops in different towns and nothing less than one hour's drive from York.'

'Burnt all the underclothing, soaked them with petrol . . . and a long way from the old house.'

'I'm glad we did it,' the man said, 'very glad. I enjoyed doing it.'

'I know you did . . . I could tell.'

'They had it easy,' the man sat at the varnished dining table, 'they would have died in the night . . . freezing to death.'

'Yes, we said so at the time . . . we told them so . . . don't worry, the pain of the cold will pass, then it will be like going to sleep . . . I still have a hunger for it.'

'So do I,' the man took a piece of bread and broke it and ate it, 'so do I.'

Hennessey followed Dr D'Acre as she knelt first by one skeleton, then moved reverentially and knelt by the next and the next and the next, as the scene of crime officers and the grim-faced constables stepped respectfully out of her way. Dr D'Acre remained silent as she inspected the chain round the ankle of one of the victims, examining the manner by which it was attached to the heavier chain that ran the length of the kitchen garden. She then examined the rope which had been used to gag each victim. 'Nylon,' she commented as she stood.

'The rope?' Hennessey replied. 'Yes.'

'Five?'

'Yes, ma'am,' he paused and then added, 'so far.'

'So far?' Louise D'Acre raised her eyebrows. She was, Hennessey once again observed, a woman who wore no make-up at all save for a trace of pale, very pale, lipstick and who wore her hair very short, and yet who, in Hennessey's eye, was very feminine in appearance and mannerism. He also once again noticed how supple and strong she was as she knelt and rose and knelt and rose, which he knew from conversations they shared over time and from photographs on her office wall had been developed because of her passion for horse riding.

'Yes, ma'am, so far. All are confined to this area, this walled garden.'

'Kitchen garden.' Dr D'Acre allowed herself rare and brief eye contact with Hennessey. 'This type of walled garden close to the main house is called the kitchen garden. It's where the vegetables would have been grown in the heyday of this estate.'

'I see . . . well, we still have to clear the garden then use dogs to cover the remainder of the grounds, but we have indication that if any more bodies are here they will be in this area . . . the kitchen garden.'

'What indications, may I ask?'

'The doorway to the kitchen garden was found to be

freed up with residual traces of lubricant, pretty well all other locks in the house and the outbuildings were found to be in a seized or at least semi-seized condition.'

'Fair enough. So regular access needed without making undue noise?'

'That's our thinking, but very early days yet.'

'For all of us Chief Inspector. Well, my early days can tell you that all five bodies are female . . . adult human female, and that they were brought here at intervals, and by that I mean intervals of many months separating each victim. They are at different stages of decay, from the fully skeletonized to the corpse over there which still has traces of scalp hair and major organs. It seems that the state of decomposition decreases the further from the doorway. See, nearest the door is the skeleton, three in fact; furthest are the corpses with residual organ remains. The overgrowth will have reduced the rate of decomposition,' she indicated towards the end of the garden, 'once you have cleared that lot you may find very well-preserved remains.'

'Yes, but we are going very slowly . . .'

'Of course . . . a crime scene . . . it has to be treated with great delicacy. I fully understand.' Dr D'Acre glanced at the skeletons. 'No obvious cause of death and they were alive when they were brought here, no point in restraining or gagging a corpse.'

'None at all.'

'Northern side of the garden, the sun would have baked them if they were here in the summer, in the sun all day, no shade, no remnants of clothing to indicate that they were clothed. If they were not kept alive they would have succumbed quite rapidly to dehydration.'

'Thirst?'

'Yes. Horrible death. What people have been known to drink because of the ravages of thirst . . . petrol . . . stagnant water alive with insects . . .'

'So I have heard.'

'If they were abandoned in the winter it would have been an easier death, very painful at first, but quick and pain free in the end,' she paused, 'but all that is pure conjecture, not scientific observation.'

'Whatever, but it does not bear thinking about, particularly the summer death, that would have taken days.'

'Yes, and all but the first would have been chained to a corpse or corpses . . .'

Hennessey asked Dr D'Acre how long she thought the corpses had been there.

'Years . . . the skeletons could be twenty years here, the fourth and fifth victims less time. They did not all disappear in a small time frame, so their disappearances might not have been linked. Is the occupant of the house implicated, can I ask?'

'No. Late occupant in fact.'

'I am sorry.'

'Ninety-seven years old . . . he had a good run . . . but he was housebound and led a hermit-like existence in the last twenty years of his life.'

'Twenty?'

'So we believe. This business . . .' Hennessey pointed to the skeletons, 'this business seems to have gone on right under his nose but in his complete ignorance.'

'So someone knew the garden existed, yet it's so far from the road and in a remote part of the Vale on top of that.'

'Yes,' Hennessey smiled, 'so we'll be tracing all the former staff . . .'

'Well, I wish you luck. Have you got all the photographs you need?'

Hennessey turned to the scene of crime officer who nodded. 'Yes, sir,' he added.

'So we can transport the bodies to the York District. I'll go and await them.' She glanced at her watch. 'I'll commence

the post-mortems tomorrow first thing, nine thirty am. Will
you be observing for the police, Chief Inspector?'

'Yes, ma'am, most probably.'

It was 16.35 hours.

TWO

Thursday 11th June – 10.05 hours – 22.22 hours
in which a home visit is made and Carmen Pharoah and
George Hennessey are severally at home to the gracious
reader.

The room was brilliantly illuminated by a series of filament bulbs concealed behind opaque Perspex sheets in the ceiling. The Perspex sheets successfully avoided the potentially dangerous epileptic fit inducing 'shimmer' and bathed the room in a bright but constant glow, which was not harmful to the eyes of those in the room. In the room, four corpses lay on four stainless steel tables arranged side by side in a row. The fifth body of the five, one of the complete skeletons, found in the kitchen garden at Bromyards remained in a steel drawer in a chilled adjacent room. 'Four is quite sufficient to start with,' Dr D'Acre had explained. A sombre mood, very sombre in fact, thought Hennessey, as he stood against the wall observing the procedure for the police. He had not known a mood more sombre to have previously descended on the room. He watched as Dr D'Acre moved the arms and legs of each body, sometimes having to use all her strength, until all four lay face up, arms by the side, legs straight out and close together, and thus affording each corpse, even in death, a degree of dignity. Each victim seemed to have expired in a foetal position, either because they had sat up against the wall as they had drawn their last breath, or more likely, thought Hennessey, having seen the five bodies shortly after they had been found, that they had, with resignation, turned on their sides and awaited their own death. Hennessey watched Dr D'Acre as she worked, moving in a slow but determined, and yet gentle, manner, using as little force as necessary and handling each corpse as if it was a living being, and so she managed to create a distinct sense of reverence for the deceased. Her eyes, too, when he was able to see them, he noted, displayed a look of respect for the dead. Her mouth was kept closed as she worked, her soft jawline set firm. A single act of clumsiness, Hennessey realized, a needless look of distaste for the work she performed, or a smile, no matter how brief, or a split-second gleam in her eyes, or of eye contact with him or Eric Filey, would ruin everything, because her attitude, her professionalism, was example setting. She was leading from the front, and Hennessey and Eric Filey were willing followers and responded by exhibiting the same decorum.

Having laid out the skeletons, with the occasional help of Eric Filey, Dr D'Acre turned her attention to the least decomposed of the four, and as such, clearly the most recent of the five bodies to have been brought to Bromyards.

'The body . . . oh, please give this a number and today's date, Kate.' Dr D'Acre spoke for the benefit of the microphone, which was attached to an angle poise that was bolted into the ceiling. 'Kate' was, Hennessey assumed, clearly a skilled audio-typist who knew what to write in the report and what not to write. It seemed clear that D'Acre and 'Kate' knew each other very well and that they worked well together. 'The body,' Dr D'Acre continued, 'is in an advanced state of decomposition and is almost completely skeletonized. It is that of an adult of the female sex. There is an absence of any significant injury to the skeleton. The skull and all long bones, ribs etcetera, appear intact. There is no sign of trauma at all.' She turned to Hennessey, 'That is worrying in a sense.'

'Yes, ma'am,' Hennessey nodded. He stood as far away from the dissecting table as possible, his place to be called forward to examine or witness something of significance only if invited to do so by Dr D'Acre. He was dressed similarly to Dr D'Acre and Eric Filey in green coveralls, including hat and slippers. They were worn over underclothing and always were incinerated after a single usage.

'Early days, yet,' Dr D'Acre returned her attention to the corpse, 'but the absence of peri-mortem trauma indicates a slow and a lingering death.' Dr D'Acre took the scalpel to the stomach, still discernible, and opened it with a single linear incision. 'Nothing in there . . . there might still have been some small trace of food even after this length of time, but its complete absence could mean that she was deprived of food in the last twelve or twenty-four hours of life . . . but decay is too advanced . . . the kidneys, too, are too decayed to be able to determine if she was deprived of fluid during the same period.' Dr D'Acre laid the scalpel in the stainless steel tray containing a generous amount of disinfectant. 'I will give all due attention to the task in hand, all due address, but if this corpse is typical of those found at the location in question, then I am obliged to give you advance warning that I am unlikely to be able to determine the cause of death.'

'Appreciate that, ma'am.'

'It's likely going to be asphyxiation, plastic bag over the head . . . or thirst or starvation . . . in lessening degrees of mercy. Asphyxiation takes a matter of minutes, thirst will take a few days . . . but if the victim is allowed fluid then starvation could take weeks.'

'We wondered about the possibility of them freezing to death?'

'Yes, hypothermia, that is indeed a fourth possibility, which will take a short time in the depths of winter and will also leave no trace upon the skeleton. Poison is an unlikely fifth, as is drowning, but those two might and will leave traces respectively. Heavy poisons such as arsenic and cyanide will leave traces, alcohol won't. But I will be able

to tell if they were drowned . . . but the absence of a body
of water in the area leads me to think it unlikely.'

'I would think so too, ma'am, the fact that they were
restrained and attached to a long chain makes me think that
they were alive when they were abandoned . . . alive and
conscious . . . from a police officer's point of view.'

'I would be inclined to agree with you, Chief Inspector,
from a forensic pathologist's point of view,' she tapped her
forefingers lightly on the rim of the table, 'from the perpetrator's point of view, I would think he'd want a rapid onset
of death . . . he would abandon them to thirst or hypothermia.
He wouldn't return each day with a plentiful supply of water
to keep them alive until they starved . . . too risky. So logic,
not scientific analysis, points to hypothermia or thirst as the
likely cause of death, depending upon the time of year they
were chained up and abandoned. But that is encroaching on
your area of expertise. Sorry.'

'Encroach all you like.'

'Thank you, but I suppose that that is my way of apolo-
gizing for being unlikely to find a cause of death. I think
my expertise, modest as it is, will be confined to doing
what I can to assist in the identification of the deceased,
especially since one victim had sustained a distinct head
injury much earlier in her life.'

'That's still very, very useful, thank you.' Hennessey
then glanced at Eric Filey and repeated, 'Thank you.'
George Hennessey had come to like Filey a great deal, and
come to respect him; young, slightly rotund, not only was
he clearly sufficiently good at his job that he impressed
Dr D'Acre but, unlike other pathology laboratory assistants whom Hennessey had met, Filey possessed a warmth
about him and approached his employment with a good-
humoured attitude, although when circumstances demanded,
as at that moment, he was capable of demonstrating sincere
reverence.

Dr D'Acre used a stainless steel length of metal to prise

open the jaw of the skeleton. 'Definitely Caucasian or white European . . . the skull is northern European in appearance, and could also be Asian, but the teeth confirm it . . . definitely northern European in terms of race . . . and there is some dental work which may prove very useful in determining her identity. As you know, dentists have to keep their records for eleven years. This particular victim was murdered, or at least lost her life, within the last eleven years. Probably in the last two or three, and the dentistry appears to be British.

So someone, some dentist, will have a record of her dental work and that is as unique as a fingerprint. Human teeth are like snowflakes . . . no two sets are ever the same.'

'That will also be very helpful,' Hennessey spoke softly, 'very helpful indeed.'

'Yes, the field is narrowing . . . no males as yet . . . and just glancing at the other skulls here, and recalling the fifth victim in the drawer, it seems that all are northern European in terms of race.'

'The field is narrowing, as you say, ma'am. We don't need to look for males or people of ethnic minority in our missing person files.'

Dr D'Acre smiled and mouthed, 'Thank you', at Hennessey and then said, 'I do like to be of some use.' She then addressed Eric Filey. 'Can you hand me the tape measure, please, Eric?'

Dr D'Acre extended the tape measure whilst Eric Filey held the tape at the head of the corpse, until it reached the feet. 'Tall lady,' Dr D'Acre commented, 'five foot ten inches, or about a hundred and seventy-eight centimetres in Eurospeak. Add an inch on to that to allow for the shrinking of the cartilage and the decay of the flesh beneath the feet, then she would have been nearly six foot in life. She was also a young woman, about twenty-five years old, no older, possibly younger.'

'Again, very useful to know, there won't be many six-feet

tall women in our mis per files. Hardly any in fact . . . and possibly just one . . . but only if she is local,' Hennessey added, 'only if she is local. I do so hope that some day we'll have a national missing person's database . . . the National Missing Persons Helpline is a charity. It has been useful in the past but we need nationally held mis per records on the Police National Computer.'

'Yes,' Dr D'Acre replied softly, 'that would make things much easier for all concerned. I am afraid I am close to completing here. All I can do now is remove one of the teeth and age it, that way I can tell how old she was when she died, plus or minus one year, and detach the skull and send it to the forensic science laboratory at Wetherby for facial reconstruction by computer modelling, so you might then have some idea of her appearance when alive . . . but as for cause of death . . . we will never know, not by post-mortem examination anyway. All information for your attention will be with you asap.'

'A very interesting patient, very interesting indeed, and very popular with the reception staff and our visiting nurses.' Dr Richard March smiled warmly at Webster as he momentarily took his eyes off the computer monitor on his desk. 'Yes, got his details up on the screen. Old boy, died of respiratory failure.'

Webster's face broadened into a smile.

'You find that funny?' March's smile faded rapidly.

'Frankly, yes, I do, but not in a spiteful way, I assure you. What I mean is . . . what I find amusing is the term because what does "respiratory failure" mean but "stopped breathing"?'

March chuckled. 'I see . . . yes, quite true, but so many relatives of elderly patients need something more than "stopped breathing" and as doctors we can't put "stopped breathing" on a death certificate, if we do then our cred-ibility is out of the window. The term "respiratory failure" gives relatives a reason for death or a cause of same . . . but as you say, all it means is that the person in question just stopped breathing. It's only used in the case of elderly people who are closely monitored up to the end . . . never on a younger, healthier person who dies suddenly. For that we have the diagnosis of Sudden Death Syndrome and in infants it is Sudden Infant Death Syndrome . . . but for geriatrics who have run their race and who die in their sleep, then "respiratory failure" it is. Mr Housecarl did contract a mild chest infection at the time of his death, but that might be because his immune system was shutting down and so allowed infection in. In the end, it was just the case that Mr Housecarl was one of those persons whose life had run its course and that was it. So "respiratory failure", though I knew he was about to die because he had had a visit . . . his brother.'

'A visit?'

'Yes, people who work in terminal care often know when one of their patients is about to expire because they will report that a predeceased relative has visited them. You'll hear it often in geriatric care, a nurse will approach her colleagues and say "Mrs Smith's just had her visit . . . she won't be long now", and sure enough, within three or four days said Mrs Smith will die quietly, often in her sleep. In just that manner, when I last visited Mr Housecarl he told me that "Tommy" had visited him. Upon enquiring who "Tommy" was I learned that Thomas Housecarl had died in New Zealand some twenty years earlier. "Tommy" had appeared to Mr Housecarl and two days later he was deceased. And patients that receive such visits are lucid, not suffering from dementia.'

'That's very interesting.' Webster sat back in the upright chair which was beside the doctor's desk and faced the doctor who sat at the desk. It was clearly the patient's chair in Dr March's surgery and was, thought Webster, a preferable arrangement to that chosen by his own doctor who kept a large desk, barrier-like, between himself and his patient.

'It is, isn't it?' Dr March, Webster found, was a doctor with a warm and cheery manner. His surgery looked out on to a brick wall, probably within reaching distance, and yet enjoyed a plentiful supply of natural light. It could not be overlooked from the outside and as such, was the only surgery that Webster had been in which did not have net curtains or some other means of preventing anyone outside from looking in on a consultation. 'Unsettling also. So what can I tell you about Mr Housecarl?'

'We need to establish the pattern of his life for some years prior to his death and also need to find his ex-employees.'

'May I ask why?'

'Yes, I can tell you, there is going to be a press release issued later today because we will need public assistance. There has been a discovery on his land; in the kitchen garden of Bromyards . . . though Mr Housecarl is not under suspicion.'

'A discovery? A dead body?' March asked with a slight smile.

'Yes, in fact. You sound like you know something, sir?'

'No, I can't help you . . . it was just a logical deduction that it would take that sort of discovery to prompt a police officer to press me for my time in a very busy day and accept being squeezed in between morning surgery and "rounds". So is that what it is . . . a dead body?'

'Yes, five in fact.'

'Five!'

'And we are still searching the garden, it's badly over-grown and so there may be more corpses to be found. It's a big case . . .'

'Oh my,' March sat forward and held his head in his hands, 'I am astounded. Years, you say?'

'Yes, sir.'

'But Mr Housecarl only died recently. You mean that all

the while myself and the nurse . . . and the Meals on Wheels folk . . . all the while that we were visiting there were bodies in the kitchen garden . . . the enclosed garden beside the house?'

'Yes, sir.' Webster paused. 'The last body was probably deposited there only a few months ago. The Home Office Pathologist won't be drawn on the time of death.'

'I bet he won't.'

'She, actually, sir.'

'She then. I tell you, the luxury of time of death being able to be determined is for TV programmes. It's very hard to determine the time of death in actuality. You know, from the time that the person was last seen alive to the time the body was found is a near as science can get to determining the actual time of death.'

'Yes, sir.'

'And corpses don't always cool either. In the tropics a body will heat up after death and will then begin to cool. That can throw a real spanner in the works.'

'Yes, sir . . . as you say. But the other victims were practically all skeletons . . . though some final victims still showed traces of internal organs.'

'I see . . . yes, I see your need to establish Mr Housecarl's life pattern.'

'We understand that in his final months he lived in just one room?'

'Yes,' Dr March pursed his lips and nodded briefly, 'yes, that was the case, and for years, not months. The last three or four years of his life he spent living in that little room, leaving only to use the bathroom opposite it. He kept himself alive by eating out of tins and on the meals the visiting catering service brought for him a few times each week.'

'He wouldn't move to a smaller house?'

'Wouldn't consider it, that was totally out of the question for him. He was fully *compos mentis* . . . remember he had a "visit" from his brother Tommy . . .'

'Yes,' Webster tapped his pen on his notepad, 'as we agreed, very interesting.'

'But the point is . . . is that he was *compos mentis* . . . couldn't enforce his relocation under the mental health legislation. He explained to me once that if he abandoned Bromyards he would feel that he was letting down his ancestry. As you may know, the house has been in the Housecarl family for nearly three hundred years.'

'Yes.'

'The original house looked different, it was smaller, a much more modest building. It was expanded during the Victorian era when the family really came into very serious money . . . but it was the same family who owned it. He felt sad that he was going to be the last of the Housecarls but he accepted that the end of each dynasty has to come some time.'

'Yes.'

'And so the least he could do, he said, was to ensure that when he does leave Bromyards, he is carried out feet first. He felt he owed that to his forebears . . . and he had everything upstairs.' March tapped the side of his head. 'In here he was as bright as a button, his body was failing but his mind was sharp and as a consequence of that, he had the right to self-determination . . . and said right we have to respect.'

'Of course,' Webster spoke softly; he felt the reverence owed to the consulting room. 'He was no harm to himself or others and Bromyards wasn't standing in the way of a proposed motorway development.'

'No . . . listed building anyway. It might fall down because of neglect but it is protected under the terms of the National Monuments Act and can't be demolished.'

'So, to confirm our belief and fully remove all suspicion, he could not, in your medically qualified opinion, be party to anything untoward which was going on outside the house?'

'No . . . not physically part of it and I can't see him giving permission for anything like that. He was a gentleman of the old school . . . a man of principle.' Dr March pursed his lips. 'No, he wouldn't have known anything about it.' March paused. 'He was a hermit for many years. He had a carer . . . an assistant . . . I met her once . . . jolly lady. Now what was her name? What on earth was it? It was a name which I thought seemed to fit her personality. Charles Dickens could have named her . . . you know how Dickens suggested the personality of his character by the names he chose for them?'

'I didn't know that.'

'Oh, yes . . . like Mr Gradgrind the schoolmaster . . . and the boy pickpocket called the Artful Dodger . . . his characters have well-suited names and this lady had a name that Dickens would have pounced on . . . what was it? Mrs Mirth . . . no . . . M something . . . she came into a room like a ray of sunshine and she was introduced and I thought how apt . . . Merryweather!' March smiled and looked pleased with himself. 'That was it, Mrs Penelope "Penny" Merryweather, and a jolly soul was she, salt of the earth . . . milk of human kindness sort of individual . . . lovely lady. She was the last of the staff at Bromyards, the last to be laid off . . . and I had the impression that she was the sort of employee who did more than her job. She seemed to have a devotion to Nicholas Housecarl. She'll be the lady to ask . . . hers will be the brains to pick about the matter of the old boy's retreat, but I think he abandoned the grounds about twenty years ago. I recall visiting about twenty years ago, when he was still living in the downstairs rooms and sleeping in an upstairs bedroom, and as I drove away I recall remarking that the hedge on the approach road . . .'

'Too long to call a drive,' Webster smiled.

'Yes, "drive" just does not convey the road from the public highway to the house, "approach road" is more apt . . . but to continue . . . as I was driving down the approach road I noticed that the privet was overdue for a trim, which it never got, and in hindsight that was the beginning of the retreat. He was letting the garden go. It was beginning then to slide into its present unkempt state. He had a few gardeners . . . head gardener and his under gardeners and the "boy", but one by one they were laid off. Then the house staff went, until only the ray-of-sunshine Mrs Penny Merryweather remained . . . and then even she too was laid off.'

'We'll have to trace her.' Webster glanced at a wallchart that showed the muscles of the human body.

'She will be a good person to talk to, I'm sure, and she should still be with us. She'll be in her sixties now, but today that's no age at all.'

'Do you know if Mr Housecarl had any visitors?'

'The meal delivery service . . . the district nurse . . . myself. There was an arrangement whereby the rear door was kept open to allow us access . . . by open I mean unlocked.'

'Risky.'

'Not without its risks, I concede, but it was not as though it was an unsecured door on a "sink estate" or on a house in a fashionable suburb. A felon wouldn't stumble across Bromyards; he'd have to know it was there.'

Webster smiled warmly, 'That's a good point, sir, very pertinent indeed. I'll pass that up to my boss.' He stood, 'Well, thank you, this has indeed been useful. So we can rule out Mr Housecarl as being a part of this.'

'Yes, I think you can. And it means that I can go to his funeral. I don't attend the funerals of all my patients but I want to attend this, although there won't be many there.'

'Where is it and when?'

'I don't know, I'll have to find that out. The funeral director is Canverrie and Son of York.'

Webster scribbled the name on his notepad.

It was Thursday, 12.17 p.m.

*   *   *

George Hennessey relaxed in his chair and read, and then re-read, the report which had been faxed to him from Dr D'Acre for his urgent attention. He read that, as Dr D'Acre had anticipated, she had not, she regretted, been able to establish the cause of death in any of the five corpses which had been found in the kitchen garden at Bromyards. Though she hoped her findings could help in identifying the victims. Each, she was able to confirm, was female. Each was an adult, although the age at death appeared to be varied, all had some degree of dental work, and all said dental work appeared to be British in nature. They were not foreign women. All were northern European in respect of their ethnicity. No personal artefacts were found on the skeletons, no rings or watches or bracelets, nor were there any evidence of clothing found, no zip fasteners or plastic buttons, for example. The latest victim had in life been a tall, young woman (her skull had not properly knitted together, thus placing her age at less than twenty-five years) probably standing about five foot eleven, or even six foot, in life. By contrast, the other four skeletons were all significantly shorter, none taller than five feet five inches when alive. Dr D'Acre's report concluded with an apology for not being more helpful.

'Still very helpful though,' he murmured as he placed the report in the thickening folder, as yet marked only as 'Bromyards – 10/6' and then glanced up in response to a gentle tap on the door frame of his office. Carmen Pharoah stood in the doorway, looking pleased with herself, Hennessey observed. He also saw that she held a manila folder in her right hand.

'DC Pharoah,' Hennessey greeted her warmly, 'do come in and take a pew.'

Carmen Pharoah walked silently on rubber-soled shoes into Hennessey's office and sat with a natural grace of movement on one of the upright chairs in front of Hennessey's desk. She glanced hurriedly out of the small window of Hennessey's office at the medieval walls of

York, then bathed in sunshine and crowded with brightly dressed tourists. She turned to Hennessey. 'We might have a match to the deceased, sir. Well, one of them, I should say.'

'Oh? I am impressed.'

'Yes, sir.' She opened the folder she carried.

Hennessey held up a fleshy hand, 'Just tell me the gist.'

'Well, sir, I read the preliminary findings in the file . . . and I thought . . . not many six-foot tall women in York . . . and the age, twenty-five years or younger . . . well, sir, to get to the point, this is the missing persons file on one Veronica Goodwin.'

'Goodwin?' Hennessey commented. 'As in Goodwin Sands?'

'Yes, same spelling . . . an "I" not a "y" and just one "n", so Goodwin . . . not Good*wynee*. Just plain Goodwin, nothing fancy.'

'Very well.'

'Well, she was twenty-three years of age when she was reported missing, about eighteen months ago. She was a Caucasian, or northern European, and stood six feet tall.'

'It's worth a bet. If I were a betting man, I would say we have the identity of one of the victims. What were the circumstances of her disappearance?'

'According to the file, sir, she went out for the night with her girlfriends and didn't come home. This was eighteen months ago . . . so winter before last . . . in the January of the year.'

Hennessey leaned forward, rested his elbows on his desk and clasped his hands together. 'You know, I think you're right, I think that we have found Veronica Goodwin, local girl, right height and age. We should have an EFIT soon; Dr D'Acre has sent her skull . . . and will doubtless be sending the other four skulls to Wetherby so a computer generated likeness can be developed. But, if there are living relatives the DNA will confirm her ID.'

'As will her dental records, sir.'

'Yes, as you say, as will her dental records. What was her home address?'

'Cemetery Road, Fulford, sir.'

Hennessey raised an eyebrow, 'Well, how appropriate.'

'Yes . . . thought that, sir.' She took a photograph from the file and handed it to Hennessey, 'Veronica Goodwin in life, sir.'

Hennessey took the photograph and studied it. He saw a thin-faced, but quite attractive, young woman with shoulder-length blonde hair, smiling confidently at the camera. The eyes seemed to exude a sense of warmth and sincerity. Importantly, her smile revealed her teeth. He handed the photograph back to Carmen Pharoah. 'Get that photograph to Wetherby by courier.'

'Yes, sir.'

'They can compare the teeth to the teeth in the skull. If they match, we have a result, a definite, positive identification of the last victim. Do that immediately.'

'Yes, sir.' Carmen Pharoah stood.

'Do you know when the photograph was taken?'

'Just a day before she was reported missing, sir.'

Hennessey and Pharoah fell silent and the poignancy reached them, being that the confident, attractive, smiling Veronica Goodwin, twenty-three years, was to be murdered within a few hours of that very convenient photograph being taken. Carmen Pharoah spoke, saying what they were both thinking, 'We just never know the minute do we, sir? None of us.'

'No . . .' Hennessey sighed, 'we never do.' Then he recovered focus. 'So who is in CID?'

'Detective Sergeant Yellich and Detective Constable Ventnor, sir.'

'All right, take Ventnor with you, go and knock on the door of the house in Cemetery Road, see what you see. Remember, no positive ID has been made yet, you'd better emphasize that. See what you see, find what you find.'

'Yes, sir.'

'I'll see what Webster comes back with before I find a job for DS Yellich.'

'Mr Yellich seems to be fighting his way through a mountain of paperwork at the minute, sir.' Pharoah turned to leave Hennessey's office.

'Imagine he is . . . but the Bromyard investigation has to take priority.'

'Two p.m. tomorrow.' Sydney Canverrie, by the nameplate on his desk, seemed to Webster to be doing very well out of the undertaking business and he further seemed to be untouched by the ever-present presence of death. He was a young man, still in his twenties, so Webster guessed. He seemed to be very well nourished, was expensively dressed in a blue suit and shirt and tie, and had what Webster thought was an inappropriately jocular attitude. He could only hope that the man adopted a more sombre manner when dealing with the distraught relatives of the deceased. The office in which both men sat was lined with light-coloured, highly polished pine wood panelling and a deep pile carpet of dark red. Canverrie's desk was large, both long and wide, and he sat in a reclinable, executive-style chair. The window of his office looked out across a neatly cut lawn to a nearby brick built building which appeared to Webster to also be part of the premises of Canverrie & Son of York. 'The deceased will be interred at Heslington Cemetery on Fordham Road after a brief Anglican service in the cemetery chapel. That is the new cemetery, not the old Victorian one.'

'Yes, I know the one you mean.'

'And it has some interest to the police?'

'Yes, it does, but we are more interested in observing who might be attending, rather than paying our respects to the deceased.'

'The old boy wasn't a felon, surely?' A note of alarm crept into Canverrie's voice.

'No,' Webster held up his hand and gave a brief and slight shake of his head, 'he appeared to have been a good man who led a blameless life, so you can bury him with all due dignity and reverence.'

'Good,' Canverrie seemed relieved, 'we would do anyway, but it's all an act . . . it's all for show.'

'It is?'

'Yes, it is all for show. It was my grandfather who started the company; my father is in fact the actual "son" of the name. The undertaking business is a display of ceremony, all very serious, but that is just the image.'

'Oh really?' Webster scowled.

'Yes, really . . . it all starts with my introducing myself to the grieving next-of-kin and saying, "Hello, my name's Sydney and I'll be looking after you today . . .", with me all dressed up in my grey pinstripe and tails with a top hat, looking every inch the Victorian gentleman or bank manager. Then I walk in front of the hearse for the first few feet of the journey to the chapel, as all the relatives and friend's cars join the convoy, and then I get into the hearse, beside the driver, and we pick up speed. So, we drop the box in the ground or hide it away behind the velvet curtains, depending on whether it's a burial or a cremation. Then we drop the rellies off at a pub where some grub has been laid on and that's our job done, then we do the next job.'

'That's interesting.'

'You think so? Damned superficial and sometimes excruciatingly embarrassing in the case of poorly attended funerals . . . one coffin and just two mourners . . . a full church or chapel and a well-attended funeral is less stressful, but I am here, for better or worse.'

'Not a happy man, I think?'

'I am here because I am expected to carry on the family business. I'd rather be a yacht broker on the Mediterranean coast, Spain or Greece, pulling down ten to fifteen per cent on every sale, and the same percentage of any charter fee

I can negotiate. So no, I am not happy in my job but I would have been disinherited if I didn't agree to sit behind this desk, cast into ye wilderness without a penny, no seed money for my yacht and powerboat brokerage.'

'I understand you are, sir, a pressed man.'

'Yes. I plan to sell the business but that will only be when I inherit it, and that won't be for a likely time.'

'How was it you were chosen to undertake Nicholas Housecarl's funeral?'

'The police called us . . . you lot. It was just our turn on the duty rota to attend to the recovery of the body and convey it to the Chapel of Rest. No one came forward to instruct another undertaker, and so we made all arrangements and will send our invoice to Mr Hoursecarl's solicitors . . . they have contacted us and asked us to do that. We have no instructions to cremate Mr Housecarl and so we will inter the gentleman's remains as is the established procedure. You can always dig up a coffin if, at some future point, a next-of-kin comes forward and instructs a cremation, but you can't un-cremate if a next-of-kin wants a burial.'

'Fair enough.'

'So we will always bury, it's the rule, always bury in the absence of a clear request from the family to cremate.'

'So, when you recovered the body from the house—'

'Amazing old building.'

'Yes . . . you didn't notice anyone taking an interest in the removal of the body?'

'No, we didn't . . . I didn't . . . it was myself and three of our employees, a police constable and the doctor. All very normal, no suspicious circumstances, natural death, old boy just expired.'

Reginald Webster walked out of the air-conditioned chill of the premises of the undertakers and into the heat of the midday sun. He made a mental note that that evening he would tell Joyce that should she ever have to arrange his funeral, she should not engage the services of

Canverrie & Son. He did not want to be planted by an uninterested man who would rather be selling yachts on the Mediterranean coast of Spain or Greece.

The Goodwin home on Cemetery Road revealed itself to be a stone-built villa, dating from the late Victorian era, within a terrace of similar houses. It had a small and neatly kept front garden which abutted the pavement. The house itself was painted white; white door and white window frames, the rest was left as naked stone. The street on which the house stood was quiet and sun drenched, causing heat hazes to rise above the asphalt surface of the road. Carmen Pharoah parked the car close to the Goodwin home though not directly outside it. She and Thomson Ventnor exited the vehicle, leaving the windows open by a matter of an inch or two, thus allowing the passenger area of the vehicle to 'breathe' in their absence. They then walked solemnly up to the door of the house of Goodwin. They stood for a moment before the front door as Carmen Pharoah turned to Ventnor and whispered, 'Here we go', and then pressed the doorbell, which made a harsh continuous buzzing sound, ceasing only when she retracted her finger.

'Prefer the "ding dong" type myself,' she commented, half turning to Ventnor, 'the ones powered with batteries rather than this type which is wired to the mains.'

'So do I,' Ventnor paused. 'In fact, I have a tale to tell about a battery powered doorbell.'

'Oh?'

'Yes, it defies logical explanation, so it's going to form the in-flight entertainment for the journey back to Micklegate Bar.'

'Sounds intriguing . . .' Carmen Pharoah's voice trailed off as the sound of a security chain was heard being unhooked from within the house.

The door was opened calmly and clearly, in her own time and on her own terms by a tall, though finely built middle-aged woman whose complexion drained of colour as she realized that Carmen Pharoah and Thomson Ventnor were police officers.

She collected herself, took a deep breath and said, 'Veronica?'

'Possibly,' Carmen Pharoah replied, she paused for a second and then added, 'in fact it's more than possible . . . we can say highly probable.'

The woman glanced downwards and then briefly closed her eyes. 'You'd better come in.' She stepped aside with a lightness of step, which both officers noticed, and allowed them to enter her home. She invited the officers to enter her front room, being evidently the 'best' room of the house, which stood to the left of the hallway. Ventnor and Pharoah entered a tidy and cleanly kept lounge containing a three piece suite of an immediate post-World War Two style, with deep seating between high-sided arms, a television stood on a mobile table in the corner of the room, a mirror hung above the fireplace and a bookcase stood in the alcove on the further side of the fireplace. The room was, thought Ventnor, very 1950s and it immediately reminded him of his grandmother's house – she had refused to redecorate her house out of respect to her husband who died tragically young in 1960. The room smelled a trifle musty through under use, being the nature of 'best' rooms in houses such as those which lined Cemetery Road, which were used only to receive respected visitors or for other special occasions. The officers were invited to take a seat and did so, sitting side by side on the settee, at either end of it, leaving a gap between them. The lady of the house sank silently into one of the armchairs, wearing an expression of fear, worry, trepidation. She rested her hands together on the lap of her green dress.

'DC Pharoah and DC Ventnor from Micklegate Bar Police Station.' Carmen Pharoah held her ID for the householder's inspection, who nodded in acknowledgement. 'Can I ask your name, ma'am?'

'Philippa Goodwin.'

'Veronica's mother?'

'Yes.'

'Is there a Mr Goodwin?'

'There was.'

'Deceased?'

'Probably, I wouldn't know, he left us when Veronica was two years old.'

'I see . . . I'm sorry.'

'Thank you, but I wasn't sorry to see him go, he was a violent drunkard. If he had not left, it would have been a messy divorce. I went back to work . . . I am a nurse . . . I was then, a nursing sister now.'

'I see.'

'So you have bad news for me?'

'You seem to know that.' Carmen Pharoah was struck by the absence of tone of query in Goodwin's intonation.

'I work in Accident and Emergency, breaking bad news is part of the job. Doctors do it and so do the police . . . nurses are on hand and so we witness it, and I have noticed that the police most often break bad news in pairs. Good news can be given by an individual officer but a pair of officers are preferred when dealing with the alternative . . . and news of long-lost relatives or relatives who were occupants of cars which have crashed is either good or bad. So, for a while now, I have known that if two police officers call at my door then they will not be bringing good news.'

Carmen Pharoah nodded briefly. It was, she thought, a fair observation, a reasonable deduction. She said, 'A body has been found.'

'A body . . .' Philippa Goodwin's voice cracked and then failed.

'Yes . . . I am afraid so.'

Ventnor remained silent. Carmen Pharoah and Philippa Goodwin seemed to him to be developing a rapport. It would, he believed, be insensitive of him to involve himself unless needed.

'The body is partially decomposed and the pathologist suggests a time of death of between one and two years ago.'

'That would fit. Veronica went missing eighteen months ago . . . winter before last.'

'And the remains are those of a very tall female in her early twenties.'

'That's Veronica . . . twenty-three and she was a tall girl, nearly six feet tall. She didn't like being tall, she would complain that it severely limited her choice of men. Women don't like partners who are shorter than they are . . . very limited sense of protection.'

'Yes,' Carmen Pharoah smiled, 'I know.'

'But you are married,' Philippa Goodwin stroked her ring finger. 'You're a tall girl and you found someone.'

'Widowed.'

'So young,' Philippa Goodwin gasped. 'I am so sorry.'

'Thank you, but we all heal. We have to. Life must go on. But, to your daughter.'

'Yes, hated being tall, especially in the north of England where people tend to be shorter than southerners . . . it was a real barrier to her finding a partner . . . only those over six feet need apply . . . so few of them, fewer unattached and even fewer are suitable in terms of social position and character.'

'I can appreciate her difficulty.' Carmen Pharoah paused. 'I am afraid you must prepare yourself for bad news.'

'Bad news? Over and above the death of my daughter?'

'Yes.'

'What could be worse?'

Carmen Pharoah paused before replying. 'There will be a press release; it will make the early evening television news and tomorrow's newspapers.'

Philippa Goodwin sat back in the armchair. 'Just tell me,'

she spoke softly, 'just tell me. She was a young woman and as a parent you fear the worst . . . and we see rape victims in A and E.'

'Well . . . I can tell you that there is no indication of any such violation. It may have happened but there is no definite indication.'

'So what then?' A note of alarm crept into Philippa Goodwin's voice.

'The bad news is that your daughter, Veronica, appears to have been one of . . . the last of a number of deceased women whose corpses . . . whose remains have all been found in the same place.'

'A serial killer!'

'So-called, yes.' Carmen Pharoah remained silent for a few seconds and then added. 'We know nothing of the existence of this man . . . or these people because they left their victims . . . or his victims . . . in a concealed location rather than leaving them to be found, as is most often the case.'

'So I have noticed . . . as if taunting the police?'

'Yes, but in this case the victims would probably have remained hidden . . . that is to say their remains—'

'Yes, I know what you mean.'

'. . . remained hidden for many years because they were left on private land.'

'Where was she found?'

Carmen Pharoah and Thomson Ventnor glanced at each other. Ventnor said, 'It'll be in the press release.'

Carmen Pharoah turned to Philippa Goodwin and said, 'In the grounds of an old house in the Vale . . . at the edge of the Wolds.'

'You mean the house owner . . . he collected victims?'

'No,' Carmen Pharoah held up her hand, 'no, no . . . he was elderly and housebound . . . he died recently. It was when an inventory was being taken of the contents of the house by a solicitor that he, the solicitor, found the remains.

They seem to have been taken there and left there in the ignorance of the householder.'

'I see.' Philippa Goodwin glanced across her living room to the window and to the cemetery that lay on the opposite side of the road to her house. 'You know, it never bothered me to live opposite a cemetery, especially one which is full and no longer used. I enjoyed the peace and quiet, especially at night. When Veronica was little we would sit in the upstairs room if there was a thunderstorm at night holding hands and looking for ghosts during the flashes of lightning . . . but now . . . those stones . . . they have a different meaning now. I dare say I'll soon be choosing a stone for her, but at least I now know what happened. I'll have her buried . . . I will definitely have her buried. I will need a grave to visit and a bit of carved granite to talk to and a little plot of land to attend to . . . make sure it's watered if there is a dry summer.' Philippa Goodwin turned to Carmen Pharoah, 'An inventory? A list of things? So Veronica was not buried?'

'No,' Carmen Pharoah held eye contact with Philippa Goodwin. 'No, her remains were exposed.'

'I always thought of her lying in a shallow grave somewhere but she was lying on the surface of the ground?'

'Yes . . . I am sorry . . . partially concealed by undergrowth but yes, lying on the ground.'

'Does it get worse? Your eyes . . . your eyes seem to be saying that there is more to come and I won't like any of it.'

Carmen Pharoah swallowed and bowed her head slightly, and then looked up at Philippa Goodwin. 'Yes, it does get worse . . . it is in the press release but it is probably better it comes from us . . .'

'Yes . . . go on . . .'

'The bodies, they were chained together . . . and the other victims were completely skeletal.'

'Oh,' Philippa Goodwin put her hand up to her mouth,

'you mean she was left chained up next to a corpse . . .'
tears welled in Philippa Goodwin's eyes, 'and clothing . . . any sign of clothing?'

'None, I'm afraid, but please see that as something
merciful.'

'Merciful? How?'

'There was no injury to Veronica's body . . . none detected
. . . and if she was left naked in the winter time, being when
she was abducted, then death would have come quickly.'

'Can I see her body?'

'I am afraid that will not be possible, her remains are in
an advanced state of decomposition and it is not the last
impression that anyone would want of their loved one, not
an image to hold in your head.'

'And speaking of which, you will have removed the head
anyway to send to a facial reconstruction expert.'

Again, Ventnor and Pharoah turned and glanced at each
other.

'I told you, I work in A and E, when there is a large-
scale disaster the police remove the hands from victims
because it's easier to take the fingerprints that way than
trying to remove fingerprints from a hand which is still
attached to the body. I did a stint in the mortuary of the
hospital as part of my A and E induction course. It's very
necessary. A and E is not for everyone but I like the crisis
management, I like the life saving bit. I wouldn't be any
good on a ward, the long term getting them better and fit
for discharge nursing, that's not for me, but if you cannot
handle death and corpses you are no good in A and E, and
so a stint in the mortuary is an essential part of A and E
induction. So I know what happens. I have assisted when
a head had to be sawn from a skeleton to permit facial
reconstruction. So you can tell me.'

'Well, since you know,' Carmen Pharoah replied softly,
'yes that has happened. It was before we found the missing
person's report, which so neatly fitted the details obtained

from the remains: sex, height, matching date of disappearance, along with the state of decomposition. We probably
did jump the gun there but the head and face were badly
decomposed. The same will be true of all known victims;
all will have their heads removed.'

'All known? You mean there may be more?'

'Yes. We have to make a thorough search, the house, the
grounds; all will have to be searched. So far we have five
known victims and we have to assume that there will be
others until we know otherwise.'

'Fair enough.'

'We still have to make a definite identification.'

'It will be her.'

'We will use dental records or DNA for that.'

'What do you need?'

'The name of her dentist and/or a sample of her hair if
you have kept her hairbrush . . . failing that . . . a sample of
your DNA.'

'You can have all three . . . our dentist is Mr Pick,' Philippa
Goodwin smiled, 'appropriate name for a dentist don't you
think? He has a surgery in Gillygate . . . and yes, I have
kept Veronica's hairbrush. It has strands of her hair within
the bristles.'

'If we could take the hairbrush with us, that will suffice.'

'You'll return it?'

'Yes, I will personally see that it is returned to you.'

'I'll let you have it before you go.'

'Appreciated. Are you happy for us to proceed on the
assumption that the deceased is Veronica?'

'Yes,' Philippa Goodwin nodded slowly, 'I am.'

'The missing person's report on Veronica states that she
didn't return from a night out with friends. Can you elaborate
on that statement?'

'Elaborate? Well, I recall the last time I saw her, I remember
that day like yesterday. The last time you see someone you
love, you never forget it.'

Carmen Pharoah smiled in response. 'You don't, do you?'

'Well . . . that day she came home from work . . . she was a telephonist . . . and she came home from work . . . it was a Friday. She looked a picture, even in her frumpy winter clothing she was still radiant. She had little to eat, she didn't eat enough especially in the winter when we need more food than in the summer, but like all young women she was figure conscious, continually weighing herself, but she was not anorexic, I saw to that. That is something else you see in A and E, young women, girls even, who have collapsed in the street or at work or at school and when you peel off their clothes for the initial examination, you find that they are nothing but a skeleton covered in skin, but Veronica was not even close to that stage. I can be a bit ferocious when I have to be and if she didn't eat at least one substantial meal and two snacks each twenty-four hours, I would get ferocious with her . . . and she knew it. So that day she ate, changed into her finery and went out with her friends.'

'Do you know the names of her friends?'

'Susan Kent.'

Carmen Pharoah wrote the name in her notebook.

'Veronica and Susan were very close, as close as sisters . . . they were school pals.'

'What is her address? We'll have to speak to her.'

'Her mother lives at the end of the street . . . that way.' Philippa Goodwin pointed to the left-hand side of her house, as viewed from the outside. 'You know, I don't know the number but it has a loud . . . a very attractive red door.'

'Loud?' Carmen Pharoah queried.

'As in colour, a "loud" colour, a colour which leaps out at you is a "loud" colour . . . apparently. That's something I learned from my husband, Veronica's father, he was an art teacher but only in his sober moments. So the Kent house has a "loud" red door . . . scarlet, fire engine red. You can't miss it.' Philippa Goodwin forced a smile. 'The colour caused comments but they still repaint it every five years.

Anyway, Susan said that she last saw Veronica waiting for a cab at the rank in the station. It's a very short journey, walkable, but for a young woman alone on a dark night a taxi is very sensible, and so Susan didn't worry about her.'

'Understandable.'

'But she didn't return home. I started to worry by about ten a.m the next morning. If she was going to stop out overnight she would have phoned me, but by ten a.m. I had received no phone call so I phoned the police. They were very sympathetic but they told me that they could not take a missing person report until the person concerned had been missing for twenty-four hours.'

'Yes, that's the procedure unless it's a child or young person under the age of sixteen.'

'They said that as well. So I went to the police station at one a.m., just after midnight, by which time she had been missing for twenty-four hours . . . gave all the details, a recent photograph and gave them Sue Kent's name and address. They agreed to visit Susan.'

'And they did. The visit was recorded but Susan Kent didn't, or couldn't, tell the officer anything that she didn't tell you . . . Veronica was last seen getting into a car, which apparently drew up at the taxi rank as though she and the driver knew each other . . . but no details . . . dark night, and the other girl Veronica was with was full of booze and couldn't tell one car from another anyway.'

'Then nothing until now, but at least I know what happened to her. She was always so sensible, such a sober minded girl, always let me know where she was. So now I know . . .'

'Yes . . . we are very sorry. Do you know of anyone who would want to harm her?'

'I don't, I'm sorry but Susan Kent might. She's married now, she's moved away from home but still in York, though.'

'We will ask her, we'll find her easily enough.'

'Veronica didn't seem troubled by anything or anyone,

just a happy young woman in her early twenties, just watching her weight and bemoaning her height and the scarcity of tall men in York . . . that was my Veronica.'

Carmen Pharoah recorded her and Thomson Ventnor's visit to Philippa Goodwin and added it to the 'Bromyards Inquiry' file, and then walked slowly home on the walls, savouring the summer weather, to her new-build flat on Bootham. She changed into casual clothes and, it being too early and too summery to remain indoors, she walked out of the city for one hour and reached the village of Shipton to which she had not travelled before. She found a small village beside the A19 surrounded by rich, flat farmland. Being disinclined to walk back to York, she returned by bus.

She showered upon returning home and ate a ready cooked meal, castigating herself for doing so, and telling herself of the importance of maintaining her cooking skills and that she should be wary of laziness, for laziness, as her grand-mother in St Kitts had always told her, 'is one of the deadly sins, chile'. Later, irritated and unable to concentrate, even on the television programmes, she retired to bed too early and thus fell asleep only to wake up at three a.m. It was then, unable to sleep, alone at night, that the demons came, flying around the inside of her head, taunting and tormenting her. She thought of her blissful marriage and the advice given to her and her husband by her father-in-law, 'You're black, you've got to be ten times better to be just as good', and how determined they were to be ten times better, she as one of the very few black women constables in the Metropolitan Police, and he a civilian employee of the same force, as an accountant. Then the dreadful knock on her door, her own inspector, 'It wasn't his fault. He couldn't have known anything,' and she was a widow after less than two years of marriage.

It was her fault. For some reason she was to blame and a penalty had to be paid, and so she applied for a transfer to the north of England where it is cold in the winter time, where the people are harder in their attitude and less giving, and are hostile to strangers . . . or so she had been told . . . and where the people can bear grudges for many, many years, and there she must live until the penalty for surviving, when her husband had not, had been paid in full.

She lay abed listening to the sounds of the night, the trains arriving and departing the railway station, the calm click, click, click of a woman's high-heeled shoes below her window, which told her all was well, and later, the whine and rattle of the milk float which told her another day had begun.

George Hennessey similarly returned home at the end of that day. He drove to Easingwold with a sense of 'something big' being uncovered, that Veronica Goodwin's and the other four skeletons were not going to be the sum. He drove through the village of Easingwold with the window of his car wound down and enjoyed the breeze playing about his face and right cheek, and as he passed the place he could not help but glance at the exact spot at which Jennifer had fallen all those years ago on a similar summer's day. He drove out of Easingwold on the Thirsk Road and his heart leapt as he saw a silver BMW parked half-on, half-off the kerb beside his house. He turned into the driveway and heard a dog bark as the tyres of his car crunched the gravel. At the dog's bark a man in his late twenties appeared at the bottom of the drive, behind a gate designed to keep the dog from wandering into the road. The two men grinned at each other. The younger man returned inside the house as the older man got out of his car and walked to where the first man had stood, so as to give loving attention to the brown mongrel that was turning in circles and wagging its tail.

Later, when father and son sat on the patio at the rear of Hennessey's house, and watching Oscar crisscross the lawn, having clearly picked up an interesting scent, George Hennessey asked, 'What are you doing . . . where?'

'Newcastle,' Charles Hennessey replied, 'representing a felon who definitely did not commit a series of burglaries during which not a few householders were injured, some seriously, despite leaving his DNA and fingerprints behind him in an easily followed trail . . . he had a crack cocaine habit, you see.'

'Ah . . .'

'The police couldn't lift him because he was unknown to them, no previous convictions, so no record of his DNA or fingerprints.'

'I see.'

'So lucky . . . but luck ran out in the form of him getting into a fight in a pub . . . nothing to do with burglaries.'

'But a recordable offence and the Northumbria Police had his DNA and fingerprints taken.'

'Yes, so they raided his home and found a number of items taken from the burglaries which he had still to sell for money for crack cocaine . . . and still he is insistent on his innocence. He's trying to convince himself, of course, as much as anyone else.'

'I know the type.'

'I bet you do . . . but will he listen to reason? So, I am instructed to fight his corner with nothing to fight it with. His story that he found the stuff in the street won't wash and, even so, that is still an admission of theft by finding . . . And you . . . your work?'

'Five murdered women?'

'Five!' Charles Hennessey glanced at his father.

'Five . . . and my old copper's waters tell me that there will be more.'

'What's the story, so far?'

Hennessey told his son the details.

'A big one.'

'Yes. We have issued a press release, it'll make this

evening's television news and tomorrow's newspapers, the press will be all over this one.'

'And your lady friend?'

George Hennessey smiled. 'Very well, thank you. You'll meet her soon.'

'We hope so . . . she sounds . . . she sounds just right for you, father. You've been on your own quite long enough. I realize now how hard it was for you to be a single parent.'

'I had help.'

'Yes, I remember, but a housekeeper is not a parent and is not a partner.'

'Jennifer was with me, I felt her presence. I still feel it.'

'Yes, that is interesting, I don't doubt you.'

George Hennessey smiled. 'Oh, she's here . . . she's here . . . I can feel her presence. She loves her garden.'

'Yes,' Charles Hennessey looked out over the neatly cut lawn to the hedgerow, which crossed the lawn from left to right with a gateway in the middle, leading on to an orchard in the corner of which were two garden sheds, both heavily creosoted. Beyond the orchard was an area of waste ground dominated by grass, within which was a pond with thriving amphibious life. 'Her garden built according to a design she drew up when heavily pregnant with me.'

'Very heavily pregnant, you arrived a few days later.'

'I remember her. I remember being on her lap and looking up at her. It's my first memory. I have continuous memory from about the age of four, islands of memory before that.'

'As is usual.'

'So unfair, sudden death syndrome.'

'Yes, just walking through Easingwold . . . on a day like today and collapsing. Folk thought that she had fainted but there was no pulse and her skin was clammy to the touch. Dead on arrival, or Condition Purple in ambulance speak . . . and you just three months old. As you say, so unfair.' Hennessey paused. 'So when do I see my grandchildren again?'

'Quite soon, they're clamouring to see Grandad Hennessey again . . . tend to think it's because you spoil them rotten.'

'Which,' Hennessey smiled, 'is exactly what grandparents are for.'

Later still, when Charles Hennessey had left to drive to his home and his family, George Hennessey made another cup of tea and carried it out to the orchard and stood where he had scattered one of the handfuls of his late wife's ashes and told her of his day . . . as he always did . . . winter and summer, and then he told her again of the new love in his life and assured her that it did not mean that his love for her had diminished. If anything, he told her, over the years it had grown stronger, and once again he felt himself surrounded by a warmth which could not be explained by the rays of the sun alone.

After sunset, and after spending a pleasant two hours reading a recently acquired book about the Zulu wars, which was already a valued addition to his library of military history, and after eating his supper and feeding Oscar, Hennessey took the dog for a walk of fifteen minutes, out to a field where he let the animal explore for thirty minutes and then man and dog returned to Hennessey's house. Hennessey then walked out again, alone, into Easingwold for a pint of brown and mild, at the Dove Inn, just one before last orders were called.

THREE

Friday, 12th June – 10.15 hours – Saturday 04.10 hours
*in which more is learned about the final victim and the
gentle reader is privy to George Hennessey's demons.*

Mrs Penny Merryweather revealed herself to be a
slightly built and a warm and a bumbling
personality. She was dark-haired and wore a ready
smile and also instantly struck Yellich as indeed having a
character which well befitted her name. She lived in a small
council house set among six other similar houses in the
village of Milking Nook. She smiled at Yellich upon him
showing her his ID and stepped aside, inviting him into her
house. Yellich entered and, following Penny Merryweather's
directions, found himself in a cluttered but neat and cleanly
kept living room where he sat, as invited, in one of the two
armchairs in the room. Yellich scanned the room and all
seemed to him to be in perfect keeping with a householder
of Mrs Merryweather's age and means. The television in
the corner was small and probably a black and white set
having, thought Yellich, the look of that vintage about it.
Framed portraits of children and adults stood along the
mantelpiece in a neat row. The wallpaper had faded and,
like the television, seemed to Yellich to belong to a different,
earlier, era. The room smelled heavily of furniture polish.
Mrs Merryweather sat in the second armchair and leaned
forward, smiling in what Yellich thought was an eager to
please and almost childlike attitude.

'Mr Nicholas Housecarl,' Yellich began, 'of Bromyards.'

'Yes, sir.'

'Deceased. Recently so.'

'Yes, sir, but you can't say it wasn't no surprise can you? I mean, his age. He did very well did the old gentleman, very well, all the village said so.'

'I understand that you worked for him?'

'Yes, sir, I was one of the staff at the big house and I was the last to leave. I was still there almost to the end I was . . . even though in the last ten or fifteen years I used to work part time, just two or three afternoons a week and none at all in the depths of winter . . . but still almost to the very end.'

'One of the staff?' Yellich settled back into the armchair. 'How many were there?'

'Oh . . . quite a few at one time, sir, quite a few . . . such a big house you see with huge gardens and grounds beyond the garden that needed looking after, not as much as gardens but looking after just the same . . . a large field of grass that Mr Housecarl had scythed once every two years.'

'Scythed?' Yellich smiled.

'Yes, sir, couldn't use a motor mower on it because of stuff laying in the grass like rotting tree trunks and so it had to be scythed. You can believe me on that one, sir.'

'How many men did that take?'

'Just the one . . . Brian Foot did that. He used to like working alone did Brian, and, with a huge field to scythe, and that he got paid when it's done, no matter how long it took to do, it suited him. It wasn't a crop you see, it just had to be cut but not gathered in. Dare say it's waist high now, but Brian wasn't on the staff, retired farmworker brought in to scythe the ten acre once every two years. He didn't gather the grass he scythed, just let it lay there to rot but that's how Mr Housecarl wanted it.'

'I see.'

'So, not only was there quite a lot of people employed by Mr Housecarl at Bromyards, but there was work enough to do that he had to hire in extra help like Brian Foot. He went before some years ago now . . . good age though . . . but not quite Mr Housecarl's age to be sure. But one by one he had to let us go . . . good days they were . . . very good days.'

'What was Mr Housecarl like as a person?'

'As a person,' Penny Merryweather exhaled and then replied in a fairly, but not hard to listen to, high-pitched voice, so Yellich felt, believing Penny Merryweather's voice might best be described as 'chirpy'. 'Well now, see . . . see . . . now what was he like as a person? He was a nice enough old boy. He did like his own way but it was his old house, I reckon fair play on that one. I like my own way in this little house of mine, so I do, but he always had time for his staff and he took an interest in us, yes he did. You see it seemed to be the case that if you worked for Mr Housecarl then he felt he had more of an obligation to you than just to pay you at a fair rate. He helped quite a few people over the years . . . someone needed a new pair of spectacles, then he'd pay for them . . . over and above paying their wage and then there was the Head Gardener . . . Jeff Sparrow . . .'

'Yes, we'll have to talk to him . . . but please, do carry on.'

'It was then that Jeff's son, his only son, fell ill while he was in Australia . . . the son that is . . . Jeff had never been more than five miles from Milking Nook in all his days, but when his son was in Australia he fell ill.'

'Oh . . . long way from home.'

'Yes, and it was the fact that he fell ill in here,' Penny Merryweather tapped the side of her head, 'in here so he did . . . mental . . . and he got locked up in a mental hospital . . . and do you know what Mr Housecarl did?'

'Tell me.'

'He only paid for Jeff to go to Australia and bring his son back to the UK, everything, airfare for the both of them plus spending money for food and rail fares and that . . .'

'Really?'

'Yes, he did that. It was just like Mr Housecarl to do that for one of his own. He got a lot of loyalty that way. There were other similar things like that he did, but what he did

for Jeff Sparrow is the biggest one. The village still talks
about it.'

'I see.'

'So the staff loved him, they did . . . old army officer
type, always in tweeds. If you got a job at Bromyards you
were in a good way of employment. He paid fair wages
but it was that he cared for his workers, took an interest in
us and was really sorry when he had to let us go one by
one, and we were sorry to have to go, especially old Jeff
Sparrow.'

'So you left at different times?'

'Yes, sir . . . at different times over many years . . . it seems
as he sort of retreated he let his staff go, old Mr Housecarl,
God rest him. I mean at first it was the grounds, so the under
gardeners went, then the garden got too much. I mean he
had staff to look after the grounds but in here,' for the second
time in the interview she tapped the side of head, 'I mean
in here he couldn't cope with the grounds. Then he couldn't
cope with the garden in his head, he couldn't, that's when
he let Jeff Sparrow go. Then room by room it all got too
much and so the domestics went, one by one, until I was
the last one. He lived in just two rooms by then. Then I
heard he just lived in one room . . . lived . . . I mean ate and
slept in one room within that huge, huge house. He was the
last of his line, you see, no more Housecarls after him . . .
not from him anyway.'

'So we understand.'

'But he didn't betray his ancestry, no he didn't. A proud
man he was, sir, principled, a real gentleman of the old
school. They say he was camping in the end, cooking on
a camping gas stove, getting Meals on Wheels a few days
each week and had a nurse looking in on him.'

'But no one bothered him?'

'Tormented him, you mean?'

'Yes.'

'No, sir. The village wouldn't have stood for it. It kept

its own children in check, sir, well in check, you can believe
me on that one, and if any youths from another village tried
to torment him then they would have been well sorted out.
They would have gone home with very sore faces; you can
believe me on that one, sir. The men of the village poached
his land, sir, tables in this village have all been laid with a
roast pheasant or a duck taken from Bromyards, but in
return, the poachers kept an eye on him. They would have
seen any strangers well off the land.'

'Poachers?' Yellich inclined his head.

'This is the country, sir, poaching happens. You hear shotguns being fired around here each day, they're not toffs
shooting clay pigeons, no they're not, you can believe me
on that one, sir.'

'Understand that, and I am not going to get anyone into
trouble for shooting a pheasant or setting a rabbit snare,
but I am interested to learn that men went on to Mr
Housecarl's land at night, and, as you say, kept an eye on
him and would have recognized a stranger.'

'During the day time also, sir. Poaching goes on twenty-
four hours. Bromyards . . . that is Bromyards estate, has been
a source of meat for this village for years now, and a source
of fruit. He has apples and pears in his orchard . . . dripping
with fruit in the season, sir. Folk didn't do no damage, they
just . . . don't know the word . . .'

'Harvested?'

Penny Merryweather smiled, 'Yes, I like that word to
describe what went on, we just harvested the Bromyard
estate for game and fruit.'

'But not vegetables?'

'None to be had, sir.'

'So no one ever went into the kitchen garden?'

'No, sir, no reason, any vegetables in the kitchen garden
would be long rotten in the ground and vegetables need
planting each year. Fruit grows each year anyway once the
tree is established. Fruit farmers have an easy time of it

compared to vegetable growers. No annual planting for fruit
farmers, just maintain their old trees and harvest every
September. Jeff Sparrow will be the man to ask about the
kitchen garden, he'll know when the last vegetables were
taken up . . . but that'll be ten years ago now. Fish too.'

'Fish?'

'Yes, he had a trout pond . . . never did taste better trout
. . . the villagers harvested that as well. Never took all the
fish, left some to keep the stock alive . . . trout can look
after themselves . . . so we had grilled trout for supper, roast
pheasant for Sunday lunch with apple pie afterwards, and
fruit in the fruit bowl, and it all came from Bromyards,
well, the estate, even venison, the poachers brought in deer
hounds to bring a deer down. All the while, Mr Housecarl
was retreating room by room. This village enjoyed good
living for the last twenty years. Now there'll be new owners,
but I dare say all good things come to an end.'

'You don't feel guilty?'

'About accepting food from Bromyards estate, you
mean?'

'Yes, that's what I mean . . . just curious . . . not being
accusative.'

'No, like I said, the village was keeping an eye on Mr
Housecarl and the poachers were careful to not ever take
too much, just what the estate could afford to give and
that benefited the estate. It keeps the game and fish
numbers healthy and the poachers would never bring
down young or male deer, just the old females . . . healthy
. . . good to eat but not going to reproduce any more.
They knew what they were doing. Like all villages, we
look after our own and Mr Housecarl and the Bromyards
estate belonged to Milking Nook so we looked after him
and it.'

'So no one harmed Mr Housecarl, but quite a few men
went on his land?'

'Quite a few, and a lot of women when the apples and

pears were ripe. Fruit harvesting has always been women's work you see, sir, you can believe me on that one.'

'Interesting.' Yellich stood. 'Thank you for your information. Where do I find Jeff Sparrow?'

The slender woman with short, close-cropped hair stood quite still and looked down at the neatly cut area of grass. She might, to an observer, have made a curious spectacle, had it not been for the fact that the small area of grass in question was within Fulford Cemetery, and had it not also been for the fact that on that summer's day the cemetery was being visited by a small number of people, each, as individuals or in pairs, also visiting a specific grave of some relevance to them. Any curiosity the woman might have attracted to herself would have been instantly evaporated as she knelt on one knee and gently laid a single red rose on the unmarked grave.

'Veronica . . .' the woman sighed as she placed the carrycot containing a slumbering newborn upon the table in the living room of her small terraced house in Holgate. The smell within the room was of warm milk and rusks and baby food. The washing machine in the kitchen whirred on its spin cycle. Carmen Pharoah had the impression that the machine was in constant use and she thought the young woman looked weary. '"Ronny" . . . sometimes she was called "Ronny" or "Ronica" . . . but how could I forget her? We grew up together . . . we were great mates in fact. Can we talk in the kitchen? He'll wake up if we talk in here.'

In the kitchen of the house Carmen Pharoah and Thomson Ventnor and Susan Boyd, née Kent, sat round a small, inexpensive metal table with a Formica top. Thompson read the room and did so quickly and discreetly, and found it all appropriate for Susan Boyd's age and situation. All the contents seemed recently purchased and 'low end', a young couple just starting out in life, just as he would expect, a newly qualified primary school teacher, his wife, and their new born firstborn to have as a home.

'I think about her often. My mother phoned and said that you had called on her. She phoned me . . .' Susan Boyd patted the small mobile phone, which was lodged amid oranges in a plastic fruit bowl on the table. 'She told me to expect you . . . asking about Ronny.'

'Yes.'

'So you have found her body?'

'Have we?'

'Well, haven't you? I mean, why else would you call?' Susan Boyd held eye contact with Carmen Pharoah and then glanced at Ventnor. 'I mean she disappears eighteen months ago, not a dicky bird is heard, police show no interest . . . just silence as the world continues to turn, then, out of the blue, the police come knocking on doors. It means there has been a development. I just hope it is not connected with the discovery out in the Wolds, the garden of that old house. It said they were chained together . . .'

'I am afraid the answer is yes,' Carmen Pharoah spoke slowly softly, 'Veronica was one of those victims.'

'The poor cow.' Susan Boyd noticed the look of surprise in Carmen Pharoah's eyes. 'It's all right,' she forced a smile, 'we used to call each other "cow" . . . "you lucky cow" . . . "you silly cow", phrases like that, but if a man called us a cow he'd get his face slapped.'

'I understand,' Carmen Pharoah smiled reassuringly. 'I realized that was what you meant, took me a couple of seconds but eventually the penny dropped.'

'Thank you. We were very close, me and Veronica.'

'Yes, both her mother and your mother said the same thing, how special you were to each other. So now we need you to help us . . . we really need your help.'

'Of course, anything I can tell you, anything I can do.'

'Good.'

'But, having said that, I remember telling the police

everything I could when we reported her . . . her mother reported her missing and told the police I was her best friend and the police visited me. I was at my mum's then in Cemetery Road.'

'Let's go over it again.'

'All right. Well, it was the last winter but one, we went out together, four girls . . . young women. We were all at that stage between leaving school and getting married, we went out "on the pull".'

'Looking for boys?'

'Yes,' Susan Boyd shrugged. 'In the event I pulled on a walk in the Dales organized by our church, it's a lot healthier than pulling in a nightclub or a pub.'

'Yes, I'll say . . . a different approach.'

'More relaxed . . . sober . . . broad daylight and there for the pleasure of the walk, much healthier. My mother-in-law belonged to a rambling club and in the book of the club's annual newsletter was a list of all the couples who had met through the club and who had got married . . . the list went back decades. In a nightclub you don't find passion, you find bodily function . . . and all the losers that you meet, no hopers and multiple divorcees.'

Thomson Ventnor winced inwardly.

'Yes,' Carmen Pharoah smiled briefly, 'not a happy hunting ground. I wouldn't go to one, but let's talk about that night . . . the night in question.'

'The night in question,' Susan Boyd echoed, 'you sound like a lawyer in a courtroom, but anyway, we went for a drink on Micklegate . . . no shortage of pubs there. Then we went to Caesar's nightclub, you get more of a younger sort there than Augusta's, Augusta's is for the older set. We got a bit of attention but no bites . . . especially not Ronny, so tall, so beautiful, but so tall. She just wasn't interested in a guy who was shorter than her, but that's where all the attention came from. So we left the club after midnight and Ronny walked away with Liz Calderwood.'

'Liz Calderwood?'

'One of the gang . . . one of the four of us.'

'You didn't go with her? You lived in the same street.'

'No, after a few drinks . . . it's just a year and a half ago but I had a different attitude then. Me and the other girl, Moira Little, we decided to slum it and went to Augusta's. We suddenly had the drunken notion of pulling a sugar daddy but Ronny and Liz had had enough and wanted to go home. They were both a right mess.'

'I see . . . carry on, please.'

'Liz and Ronny left to walk to the railway station to get a taxi for Liz, who is very small and because of that very vulnerable, so Veronica was going to walk her there. She was going to see Liz safe into a taxi and then walk home. The railway station to Cemetery Road is no distance at all.'

'Where can we find Liz Calderwood? We'll have to speak to her.'

'Liz . . .' Susan Boyd grimaced, 'Liz . . . poor Liz. She went off the rails big time . . . I mean, big style.'

'Oh?'

'Yes, she married but did so badly, her man led her into a life of crime, she's inside.'

'Prison?'

'Yes. So you'll have all the details you need.'

'As you say,' Carmen Pharoah and Thomson Ventnor glanced at each other. 'Makes things easier for us,' she said.

'Much,' Thompson replied, 'much easier.'

'She's in Langley Vale.'

'Convenient.'

'So, no one paid Veronica any attention in the nightclub, or earlier in the pub.'

'No.'

'And you'd know if she had any such attention?'

'I'm sure she would have told me. She never mentioned any problem like that. She was quiet when sober but when she had a drink in her she got talkative. It's then she'd blurt something out, as she once did. She had an abusive boyfriend once. I only found out because she told me when she'd had a few rum and cokes. He knew how to hit her so she wouldn't show any bruising . . . fist to her scalp . . . he'd raise lumps on her head. I ran my fingers through her hair that night, it was like feeling a cobbled road surface, but she had such a fine head of hair that it never showed. He was clever like that.'

'What was his name? Do you know?'

'Piers Driver.'

Thomson Ventnor wrote the name in his notebook.

'She was well finished with him before she went missing though.'

'Even so, it's a stone we'll have to turn over. Violent men are often very possessive.'

'OK, but in the event, it was more like he left her. He found another punchbag he liked better than Veronica.'

'I see. That's another feature of the possessive person-ality, they can discard "possessions" very quickly, espe-cially if acquiring a replacement, but please, carry on.'

'It seemed that the only thing that Veronica liked about Piers Driver was that he was taller than her, her one big weakness, and it made her fall for a street rat like Driver.'

'I am beginning to understand her need,' Carmen Pharoah glanced out of the kitchen window at a backyard and the roof tops of black terraced houses that formed the adjacent street, 'but we'll still have to interview him again. You see our point of view, someone who used her as a "punch bag" prior to her disappearing, he sounds interesting.'

'Yes. I don't know where he lives though and I don't want to know, but you know him.'

'Sounds like the sort of person we would know . . . Piers Driver. . . . in his twenties?'

'Yes. York boy.'

'OK. Anything else you think we ought to know?'

Susan Boyd turned and also looked out of the kitchen

window, then she slowly returned her gaze to Carmen
Pharoah. 'Well, I don't know if it is relevant but Veronica
had a bit of a drink problem.'

'She did?'

'Yes . . .'

'How big a problem?'

'I think it was quite serious. She hid a flask in her handbag
and took nips to add to the drinks she bought, or would go
to the toilets and return looking a bit glazed.'

'I see.'

'She was worried about her job. She had had a warning
from her boss at work.'

'Really?'

'So she once told me, but that was a blurt out assisted by
alcohol, as well. She wouldn't have told me if she was sober.
It still didn't stop her going out at night, and especially each
weekend, but she didn't stay in during the week. So it was
getting hold of her but the thought of getting the chop at
work was a real scare for her. I mean, she was for the
shredder if she didn't get her act to together.'

'Interesting.'

'You think it's relevant?'

'It could be, it would certainly make her vulnerable.
Where did she work?'

'Gordon and Moxon's.'

'The department store?'

'Yes. Well, it's more of a household goods store, everything for the householder. Veronica worked in the city centre
branch, the main one. It's a chain organization and has many
shops in the north of England.'

'So I believe.'

'I don't know any details; I mean any details about what
made her fear losing her job. What happened that they felt
they had to give her a warning, she didn't tell me, but it
had to have been serious, affecting her performance.'

'How long before she disappeared did she tell you that?'

Susan Boyd sank back in the inexpensive metal chair upon which she sat and once again glanced out of the kitchen window. 'Well, I remember light nights, we were in the pub, we had been in there all evening and the curtains were open. I remember a lovely sunset . . . so summertime, it would be the summer before she disappeared.'

'So about two years ago?'

'Yes,' Susan Boyd nodded gently, 'yes, it would be about two years ago. But she kept her job so she pulled herself back from the brink.'

Somerled Yellich thought that Jeff Sparrow could best be described as sinewy. Yellich saw a man who was slender yet muscular, with a leathery, weather-beaten, tanned complexion, a man who had spent his working life outdoors. Jeff Sparrow occupied a similar house to that of Penny Merryweather, small, council owned, on a small estate of similar houses in Milking Nook. It had not the softness of Penny Merryweather's house, but rather Yellich found it to have the harder, more functional character of a single man's house. The mantelpiece, though, contained framed photographs of a younger Jeff Sparrow with a wife and a son, and spoke of happier, more fulfilled times. Sparrow sat in an armchair and his legs were of such a length that they inclined steeply from his waist before his calves fell vertically into the carpet slippers that encased his feet. He wore an old blue shirt with the sleeves rolled up and a pair of equally aged lightweight summer trousers. The interior of the house had a slight mustiness about it, so Yellich found, and thought that should she be so inclined, Penny Merryweather could do much for Jeff Sparrow in terms of housekeeping. The small garden of the house was neatly kept as, Yellich thought, fully befitted a head gardener (retired).

'Lonely man,' Sparrow had a soft but distinct accent of the Yorkshire Wolds.

'Mr Housecarl?'

'Yes. Who else? A lonely man. Lovely man but very lonely, very on his own. I got the impression that was what he had got used to rather than how he wanted it to be. But a lovely man just the same.'

'Yes, Mrs Merryweather told me what he did for your son.'

'For me and my son . . . but yes . . . what other man would pay for his gardener to go to Australia and collect his son from an institution and bring him home? Lovely man. We . . . his staff, just couldn't do enough for him when I told them what he had done, the village too. He was worshipped in this village. If ever a position became vacant at Bromyards, in Mr Housecarl's employment, a queue would form.'

'I see. How is your son now?'

'Very ill, but thank you for asking, sir. He has something called "paranoid schizophrenia with complications", so the consultant told me. He's in a flat in a housing association tenancy in York. It has a controlled entry so that gives him some protection, and he gets an injection of his medication each week which keeps him . . . level . . . but that's not the right word, that's not the word the consultant uses.'

'Stable?' Yellich suggested.

Jeff Sparrow smiled. 'Yes, that's the word he used. And because he has his medication injected they know he takes it. I often think it's like pruning or pollarding a fruit tree, or making sure a lawn is very closely cut, stopping the wild thing inside from growing. It keeps him acceptable, like a well-cut hedge. It's just the way I think. I've never been anything but a gardener . . . left school to become an under gardener at Bromyards. So it's the way I think.'

'Understandable.'

'But he'll always be ill, poor lad, he'll always be a hedge that needs trimming, but he likes the nurse who visits and the other help that's been linked in, someone to help him do his shopping. I call round but I know he's embarrassed about his situation so I don't visit too often. He had his breakdown in Australia and they put him in a hospital which was run like an army camp, where the patients had to address the nurses as "sir", but we got him home . . . me and Betty had him back. Betty is deceased now but she lived to see him home and settled in his flat, all thanks to Mr Housecarl.'

'I'm sorry.'

Jeff Sparrow opened the palm of his right hand. 'It can't be helped, and she was the sort of woman who would have let Tom be a burden to her, even in her autumn years. It's best that he's as independent as he can be.'

'I know what you mean,' Yellich smiled. 'I have a son who has special needs, he'll always be vulnerable, never have a mental age of more than twelve years. He'll always be dependent to some degree.'

'I'm sorry to hear that, sir.'

'Well, what can I say? We . . . my wife and I, were disappointed of course, but he gives us so much. He's so warm and generous and a whole new world has opened up to us, and for us, as we have met other parents with Down's Syndrome children.'

'I know what you mean, sir. You know I loved my son more when he became ill. I just don't want him to be a future prime minister any more . . . or an international sportsman.'

'I feel the same. So, Bromyards . . .' Yellich brought the conversation back on track but he sensed he had developed a rapport with Jeff Sparrow. He sensed he had made an ally.

'Aye, Bromyards . . . the bodies. I saw the television news last night . . . a rum do.'

'You wouldn't know anything about that?'

Jeff Sparrow smiled. 'No, it's ten years now since I left Bromyards. Mr Housecarl just shrank back into the house, lost interest in the garden. They tell me that he was living in just one room at the very end, poor old soul.'

'He was,' Yellich nodded and committed the 'ten years' to memory. It meant none of the remains could have been there for more than ten years.

'I just don't like that thought, the thought of him dying like that. Once he lived in the whole house and saw to it that the gardens and grounds were well tended. Then one by one the staff were let go, and he was generous, each man or woman got a year's pay as a . . . there's a word . . .'

'Severance pay?'

'Possibly that's it . . . but a whole year's money. Generous . . . I used my money to help Tom furnish his flat.'

'Good of you.'

'Well, there's no pockets in a shroud.'

'Indeed. So tell me about the kitchen garden.'

'That was one of the last places to be abandoned. The lawn in front of the house was *the* last part of the garden to be tended to, the kitchen garden was the next last as I recall.'

'Did it have a lock on the door?'

'Yes it did, it was always kept well-greased against the elements but it was never locked. I mean, who's going to walk a mile from the road to steal some carrots and walk a mile back? No need ever to lock the kitchen garden.'

'So anyone could enter?'

'Yes.'

'Who would know it was there?'

'All the estate workers . . . whether gardeners or domestics . . . they collected the vegetables.'

'The domestics dug them up?' Yellich was surprised at the notion.

'No, we planted them, we dug them up when they were ready and stored them, the domestics collected them from the vegetable cold store.'

'I see.'

'It wasn't a secret garden like in a children's storybook.'

'Could it be overlooked from the house?'

'Not fully if I remember. If you stood by the door of the garden you could see the upper windows of Bromyards just above the far wall of the garden. So I would say that about two-thirds of the garden, that is the two-thirds nearest the house, could not be overlooked from the house.'

'Got you.'

'But I took up the last vegetables just before I left and then closed the door behind me. The old garden just got overgrown I suppose . . . well, it would have done.'

'Did you ever return to the house?'

'Bromyards? Yes, I did. I used to walk up there to look at the gardens. I put my life into those acres, there's a whole lot of me in that soil. So, yes, I used to walk up there, not so often now, but newly left I went up each week to walk the grounds. A lot of folk went to poach and I'd often meet someone I knew with a pair of hares slung over his shoulder . . .'

'Yes, Penny Merryweather told me that the estate became a good source of food for the village. She's worried now, new owners will be moving in.'

'Yes, we all see the end of a good time coming. I didn't poach myself but I had a bit of cheap meat over the years, a good bit.'

'So there were plenty of visitors to the estate?'

'Yes . . . dog walkers too . . . it was a good place to take a dog and let him off the lead . . . let him go exploring the grounds. More fun than letting him run on a playing field. Mind you, they were lucky not to snag a snare, but if they did, the owner was on hand to free them.'

'Did you ever see anybody you didn't recognize on the estate, anyone acting suspiciously?'

'Just once.'

'What . . . who did you see?'

'Tall bloke . . . very tall . . . just looking about the grounds but he was nowhere near the kitchen garden though.'

'No matter,' Yellich reached into his pocket for his notebook, 'tall man you say?'

'Yes. Six feet tall, probably more . . . heavy set . . . he caught my eye because he was a stranger and he wasn't walking a dog and he wasn't poaching.'

'No?'

'No, sir, no dog, and he was too brightly dressed for poaching . . . and he crashed through the shrubs. No poacher would make that sort of racket; he'd have sent every pheasant and duck for miles around into the air, and every rabbit or hare down into their burrows. He was interested in the grounds, though he didn't seem interested in the house. He wasn't a burglar.'

'That is very interesting, very interesting indeed.' Yellich made notes.

'Yes, I thought it was a bit funny . . . you know "curious" . . . if that's the word. It certainly sank into my mind and it has stayed there these ten years.'

'Ten years?'

'About that . . . I was newly laid off and visiting Bromyards quite frequently, couldn't separate from the estate very easily, had to keep returning in the early days . . . of retirement that is.'

'I see.'

'He probably didn't know he was being watched, townies never do. Moving about . . . no attempt to camouflage himself . . . no green jacket . . . but I saw him and watched him close. '

'The fields have eyes and the woods have ears?'

'Yes, that was it. Only a townie would think he wasn't being watched if he didn't see anybody around him. A countryman would assume eyes are on him all the time. There is great truth in the expression you just used, sir.'

'Did you see a car?'

'No, no I didn't . . . but he would have needed one. There isn't a bus service to speak of . . . isn't now and there wasn't then. Two buses a day into York and two back again, it's the York to Driffield service, they run about once an hour but four times a day, a bus takes a detour into Milking Nook . . . two going to York, two going from York . . . and they alternate, in-out in-out . . . but that man was a car owner, he had the look of money about him, he wasn't worried about the time.'

'The time?'

'Missing the last bus. If you miss the last bus you are stranded in Milking Nook or York until the next day, unless you miss the last bus in or out on Saturday, in which case you are stranded in either place until Monday morning, depending which way you are travelling.' Jeff Sparrow paused. 'You know, I think there is something else as well. He must have known about the estate. I mean about Mr Housecarl abandoning the grounds and the garden. He seemed to be on a recce mission.'

'That's a good point, a very useful observation,' Yellich smiled. 'That could help a lot.'

'It could?'

'Yes, I would think so . . . a stranger who knew that the grounds and garden of Bromyards had been recently abandoned but not the house itself. Yet all the employees of the estate, the gardeners and the domestics, all live in the village. And no sign of a car?'

'None, but he could have left it in the village and walked to the estate. He seemed a fit man.'

'Age . . . about?'

'Middle-aged . . . possibly fifties.'

Yellich tapped his notepad. 'You say that the driveway to the house from the public highway is a mile long?'

'Yes, sir.'

'Was he near the driveway?'

'Yes, he was, as I recall, not on the driveway itself but

only a few yards from it . . . about fifty yards when I saw him.'

'How far along the drive?'

'About halfway.'

'So he was well inside the estate grounds?'

'Yes, well inside, a definite trespasser.'

'I see . . . and appreciate it's going back ten years now . . . but was there any direction to his interest?'

'Seemed to me that he was going towards the house, he was in no hurry but he was making for the house.'

'All right,' again Yellich paused, 'and you know of no employee of Mr Housecarl who lives in York . . . Driffield?'

'No, but we all know people outside the village. I know my son who lives in York, like I just told you, and also another elderly couple, but just on Christmas card terms, that would most likely be the case for all the villagers. One would tell someone about Bromyards and he would tell someone else, the news would get out . . . not just to York or Driffield but to all the neighbouring villages as well.'

'Yes, it's the sort of news that would travel.'

'And it did travel. We got boys coming to try their hand at poaching the grounds, till our village boys put them right about just who owns Bromyards . . . from a poaching point of view that is.'

'So, a tall man in his fifties knew about the abandoning of the grounds but also about there not being an imminent sale of the property,' Yellich pondered aloud.

'Possibly . . . just the ideal sort of place to hide a few bodies, but that is for you to say, I'm a retired gardener not a retired copper . . . but if I were to hide a body or a couple of bodies, I would go as near the house as possible and the kitchen garden would be ideal.'

'Oh?'

'Yes, the poachers didn't go near the house out of respect for Mr Housecarl, they didn't want to alarm him by firing shotguns under his window. It seemed like there was an agreed "no man's land", a zone round the house about a quarter of a mile wide, no one poached inside that zone.'

'So no poacher would go near the house, let alone into the kitchen gardens?'

'That's right. Ideal place to hide a body or two, but they'd be found eventually . . . had to be . . . once Mr Housecarl died, they'd be found.'

'As you say. Can you describe the man you saw?'

'Not in any detail, I was three hundred yards away, but tall, like I said.'

'Beard, spectacles?'

'No to both . . . clean shaven, no spectacles. Well built . . . muscular rather than overweight, as I recall. Important that you remember we are going back ten years, so can't be sure how accurate the description I give is.'

'Understood.'

Tang Hall Housing Estate, York YO11, was a development of medium rise slab-sided buildings in the tenement-style favoured in Scotland and Europe; an area where old cars were parked in the street and powerful motorbikes were chained to lamp posts, and the Pike and Heron public house, in the centre of the estate, was the only hostelry. The Pike and Heron was rough on the outside and rougher on the inside. It was brick built in an angular, flat-roofed-style and was known locally as 'The Fortress'. Inside 'The Fortress' Carmen Pharoah and Thomson Ventnor sat opposite Piers Driver. The hum of conversation that had ceased when Pharoah and Ventor entered had, by then, resumed at a lower volume, but the two officers continued to invite hostile looks.

'You're quite happy to be seen talking to the likes of little us in here?' Ventnor asked in a hushed tone. 'We could arrest you and take you in for questioning if that would look better.'

'We need information,' Pharoah added, 'so the last thing

we want to do is make things difficult for you. People seen talking to cops on this estate have been known to wake up in hospital.'

'That depends on who you talk to and what you say,' Driver growled. 'It's OK; they know I won't be grassing anybody up.' Driver was a tall man, as Susan Boyd had described. He had a hard, lined face, short black hair, tattoos on his neck and hands. He sat in front of a half-consumed glass of lager which stood on a circular table that was sticky with spilled alcohol. 'But they'll still want to know what you wanted. It'll be about Veronica.'

'Yes,' Carmen Pharoah said, 'yes, it is. We understand that you knew her . . . Veronica Goodwin of Cemetery Road . . . that Veronica . . . just to be certain we are talking about the same person.'

'Yes, I meant her. She's been found.' Driver nodded to the television set perched high on the wall in a corner of the room, which at that moment was showing motor racing with the sound turned down. 'I watched it on the news . . . at home there's a lot of coverage, can't miss it . . . not here; here it's always sports, always with the sound turned down, unless it's an important football match or something like that.'

'Yes, she was found along with a few other women.'

'I saw that too . . . chained together but died at different times . . . that is weird.'

'But you knew her?'

'Yes.'

'You were prosecuted for assaulting her.'

'No, I wasn't. You should check more thoroughly. Yes, I have previous for assault but not against her, I was too fly.' Driver grinned at Ventnor and withdrew his attention from Carmen Pharoah.

'It has been said that you were quite free with your fists.'

Driver leered. His flesh seemed to the officers to be ingrained with dirt, he wore a baggy tee shirt which also seemed in need of a wash, as did his jeans which were sufficiently faded that they were nearer white in colour than their original blue. His feet were encased in torn red and yellow sports shoes. His nicotine-stained fingers spoke of heavy smoking and his missing front teeth and heavily scarred left jaw line spoke of street violence. 'It was for her own good.'

'And where have I heard that before?' Carmen Pharoah said quietly and wearily.

Driver glared angrily at her once and then forgot her again. His attitude said that he was a man who did not like women in general and he particularly did not like Afro-Caribbean women, and very especially did not like them if they were police officers. 'It was though, for her own good I mean.' He gasped and Ventnor received a blast of alcohol laden breath mixed with halitosis.

'Meaning?'

'Meaning that she had a problem.'

'A problem?'

Driver flicked his index finger at the glass of lager so that the nail struck it causing a soft 'ping'. 'A problem with this.' Driver shrugged. 'All right, so I take a drink when I can afford it . . . but with her it was a problem, a real problem.'

'Oh?'

'Yes, a very serious problem. You've visited her mother in Cemetery Road?'

'Yes, of course, but she didn't mention anything about a problem with the booze.'

'She wouldn't. I mean, she wouldn't would she, even if it meant finding her killer? She . . . Veronica . . . she was her only daughter. In her eyes she was little Miss Perfect, even if she is just kidding herself on, just to keep the memory of Veronica that she wants to keep, not the memory of who she actually was. But take it from me, pal, she had a problem. She hid it quite well but she had a problem that she could not hide forever. You know, some of the people all of the time . . . and all the people some of the time . . . but she couldn't hide it from all of the people all of the time, though she tried to.'

'Secret drinking?'

Driver nodded. 'Voddy . . . she was one for the vodka. It suited her if she was hiding it from herself as much as other people.'

'No hangover, you mean,' Ventnor suggested. 'Is that what you mean?'

'That's it. Spend the evening drinking red wine or stout and in the morning you feel like your head is being crushed by a steamroller, but spend the night on vodka, you wake up the following morning feeling like you had a dry night. She could get up for work each day you see, and, if she stayed in in the evening, she'd have a bottle in her room and hide the smell on her breath with toothpaste so her old mother never cottoned on, or if she did, she ignored it.'

'I see.'

'So I smacked her a few times . . . gave her a slap, like where it wouldn't show. I was trying to scare her into not drinking but it didn't do no good . . . all her money went on voddy. She hadn't got hardly any left to buy my lager . . . and that was more important.'

'You think so?'

'Well, I'm the man, she's the woman . . . she was the woman . . . we need it, they don't. It's the way it is. Ask anyone in the pub. That's why all the punters in here are men, it's because the women are at home . . . stands to reason. And anyway, she was working, I wasn't, she had to buy me beer, but she couldn't buy me beer because she spent her money on vodka so I slapped her around a bit. It was for her own good.'

'Or for your beer, not her own welfare?'

'Same difference. Alcoholics Anonymous was no help to her, no help at all.'

'She went to AA meetings?'

'Yes, but like I said, no good it was. She just didn't want
to stop, see? They all say the same thing; you've got to
want to stop and Ronny . . . she just didn't want to stop . . .
not at all. She'd sooner go without food than go without
vodka. I mean, she just didn't know when to stop, did she?'

'I don't know,' Ventnor replied icily, 'didn't she?'

'No, she didn't.'

A large man in an unironed white shirt and white summer
trousers suddenly broke away from a group of men who
had been standing at the far end of the bar and ambled
slowly but purposefully over to where the officers and Piers
Driver were sitting. 'All right here are we, pal?' he growled
menacingly.

'Yes, boss. These be the law.'

'I know,' again said with a menacing growl.

'They want to know about Veronica Goodwin . . . that lass
I knew . . . she was one of the women found in the grounds
of that big house in the Wolds, been all over the news.'

'That's all?'

'Yes, boss.'

'All right then.' The man turned and walked back to the
bar, and as he approached, the group of men parted to allow
him access. He reached out a meaty paw and wrapped it
around his beer glass and was heard to say, 'Seems all right,
but watch him anyway.'

'Yes, boss,' two of the men answered simultaneously.

'So we split up, me and her,' Piers Driver continued, 'and
that was that. She went her own way and I went mine. Then
I heard she had vanished into thin air . . . about two years
ago. Mind you, I had hooked up with another chick by then
. . . a real player.' Driver grinned at Thomson Ventnor.

'You mean she had plenty of money to buy you drink,'
Ventnor responded coldly.

'Yeah . . . she still does,' Driver replied with a wink. 'She
still does.'

*   *   *

'She was indeed a very pleasant, a most pleasant young woman.' Megan Farthing revealed herself to be a warm, motherly sort of woman, or so found Carmen Pharoah who was relaxing very quickly in her presence. Megan Farthing was warm of manner, gentle of speech and seemed comfortable to be in her middle years, wearing a three-quarter length skirt and a 'sensible' pair of shoes and a richly embroidered blouse. She sat behind the desk in her office on the top floor of Gordon and Moxon's Household Goods Store. 'We were all saddened to hear of her disappearance and frankly, after a few days, we all expressed doubts that she would turn up alive. Young women like her don't run away, so we began to think that she'd be at the bottom of the river . . . now we know what happened to her, poor girl. So young, so much to live for . . . it was all ahead of her.'

'What was she like as a worker?' Carmen Pharoah sat back in the chair which stood in front of Megan Farthing's desk.

Megan Farthing smiled a tight-lipped smile, 'Well . . . she was an employee with an issue . . .'

'Oh?'

'Yes . . . she was pleasant, well liked . . . not a management problem but she had an issue with alcohol which surfaced eventually.'

'She came to work drunk?' Carmen Pharoah gasped.

'No . . . no . . . she never did that . . . but she left in that condition. She had a flask in her handbag.'

'I see.' Carmen Pharoah glanced round the office and thought it softly decorated and homely, with photographs of children and infants above a bookcase which stood against the wall of the office, a glass vase on the desk contained flowers in water, behind it on the wall were prints of Yorkshire landmarks, Robin Hood's Bay, the Ribblehead Viaduct, York Minster, and a sweeping panorama of Swaledale.

'You see, Veronica would bring a flask to work each day concealed in her handbag, as I said, and she would be a very efficient employee in the forenoon but she became more unsteady as the day wore on. By lunchtime she'd be taking sufficiently frequent trips to the ladies toilets to take a nip . . . and by the early afternoon she'd be walking unsteadily on her heels and slurring her words. Now . . . this is a good company to work for, it was founded in Victorian times and has resisted takeovers from larger chains which do not care for their workers as we care for ours. We have retained the Victorian attitude of paternalism to our workers. If you work for Gordon and Moxon's it works for you . . . you belong to the family . . . it's a very good employer. If an employee cannot work for an extended period through no fault of their own we will hold their position open for them. If they require money for things like school uniforms we will issue an interest-free loan and take the money back a little bit each week or month, and in such small repayment amounts that the employee won't feel it . . . financially speaking.'

'Not bad.'

'Not bad at all . . . and we do other similar things for our own, but at the end of the day we have to make money and so we have to have workers, not passengers. Veronica was one of the telephonists and as such she was in direct contact with the public . . . paying customers . . . voice only but that is still direct contact.'

'Of course, it's vital for the telephonists to have a pleasant speaking voice.'

'Yes . . . Veronica had, in the forenoon, and only in the forenoon. In the afternoon her voice was slurred and she became short-tempered. So . . . verbal warning at first, given by me in my capacity as Personnel Manager, and then when she didn't alter her ways . . . or when she could not . . . because I understand alcoholism . . . I have had personal experience of it.'

'I see . . . I'm sorry.'

'Long time ago now but it gave me insight into the illness.' Farthing paused. 'Well, anyway, she received a second written warning and strong advice that she seek help from her doctor or by joining Alcoholics Anonymous. She was then taken from the switchboard, for everybody's sake, and given a job in the stores on a reduced income . . . and that was a real comedown for her. The stores have invited some very cruel names from the workforce. "The bat cave" being one of the kinder ones. It's where the disadvantaged people work. Again, it's Gordon and Moxon's policy to engage people who would, for one reason or another, find it difficult to get a job but we can't put them on the sales floors.'

'Appreciate that.'

'So our senior store clerk is a man who is in a wheelchair because he was born without legs, and damned efficient he is too. Another employee has a glandular problem and rapidly starts to smell of sweat. He has to bring a change of clothing with him each day and take a shower at lunchtime. He's also a very good worker. And so taking Veronica from the switch-board, where the telephonists regard themselves as a bit of an elite in the company, and sending her to the stores, was a massive comedown for her but it was the only thing I could do, short of dismissing her, and I also thought it might be the jolt, just the sort of wake-up call she needed.'

'I was thinking the same thing.'

'And if she sobered up, we'd have her back on the switch-board . . . and I told her that. But it was just about then that she disappeared. She'd been in the stores for less than a month . . . and the tragedy of it was that she seemed to be getting on top of her drink problem . . . she was on her way back to the switchboard, so no reason to run away.'

The agent's room in HM Prison Langley Vale was square in terms of floor area, about eight foot by eight foot, guessed Thomson Ventnor, who sat at a metal table. It smelled strongly of bleach. The walls were tiled with glazed white and blue tiles, which had been laid alternating with each other laterally, and which had been offset like bricks in a wall. A filament bulb behind a Perspex screen in the ceiling illuminated the room. An opaque glass brick at the top of the outside wall opposite the door allowed in ultraviolet light. Ventnor heard the jangling of keys and the opening and shutting of a large, heavy door, then the agent's room door was unlocked and opened.

Liz Calderwood was dressed in a blue tee shirt, faded blue denims and white sports shoes. She grinned at Ventnor as she entered the agent's room and, unbidden, sat down opposite him. She was small, frail, innocent-looking and, thought Ventnor, she could pass for a fourteen-year-old. He saw at once how her charm and innocent-looking appearance would help her defraud gullible people, which she had done, and for which she had collected three years' imprisonment.

'Yeah . . . I heard,' she replied in a soft voice after Ventnor had explained his reason for visiting. 'We get the television news to watch and the newspapers to read and so, yeah, I heard about her being found . . . one of a number of women. Nine bodies it is now. Nine. I saw the latest press release. I did wonder what she was doing. Now I know.'

'We understand that you were the last person to see her alive?'

'No,' Liz Calderwood smiled and showed that her eyes had a most un-criminal like sparkle about them. 'No, that was the person who murdered her. Point to me I think.'

'Point to you, agreed,' Ventnor inclined his head in acknowledgement, 'but of her friends and acquaintances, you were the last known person to see her alive. You left the nightclub together, we understand?'

'Yes . . . that is true . . . I remember it well. I didn't drink as much as she did so I can remember things that happened and I can remember that night all right . . . like it was yesterday. She was a mess . . . Veronica was a mess. She was drunk and she had vomited in the washbasin in the ladies toilets, it was in her hair . . . it was on her clothes . . . everywhere . . . her tights were torn. She was mumbling about having to get home and rinse her hair but she didn't want her mother to see her. So we walked. Well, she stumbled and I held her up, even though she was taller than me, and we got to the railway station to try to use the toilets in there to clean her up but by then they had been locked up for the night . . . so we hung around. Her old mum would go to bed at midnight she said and it was well after that by this time. So she planned to sneak in quietly, wash her hair and get some sleep. She was tired and that, plus the booze . . . well you can imagine what a handful she was . . . and she still kept taking nips from her flask. There were no cabs but eventually a car stopped . . . I don't know whether it was a cab or not but I got the impression the driver knew her.'

'That could be significant.' Ventnor leaned forward and rested his elbows on the table to. 'Did you see the driver?'

'No . . . it was dark.'

'Recognize the car?'

'No . . . I'm an "all-cars-look-the-same-to-me" merchant. I seem to recall that it was a dark coloured car but can't be clearer than that. So I helped . . . no, I poured her into the car and that was the last time I saw Veronica Goodwin.'

Reginald Webster sat heavily and resignedly into one of the chairs in front of George Hennessey's desk. He held a number of manila folders in his hands.

'You've had some luck, I think.' Hennessey put his pen down.

'Yes, sir, I believe that I have matched seven of the nine bodies now known to have been found in the kitchen garden to missing person's reports.'

'Good.'

'Not a difficult job, there are not many mis per reports of females in the Vale, not of the age group we are talking about and helped in the case of Gladys Penta by a disfiguring head injury she had sustained earlier in her life . . . the result of a climbing accident in fact.'

'You look puzzled Webster.'

Webster forced a smile, 'Does it show?'

'It shows,' Hennessey replied. 'So what is it?'

'It's their ages, sir . . . the ages of the victims.'

'Oh?'

'That is, if they are who I think that they are, we still have to confirm the identity in all the cases, only Veronica Goodwin is confirmed up to now.'

'Go on.'

'Well . . . the female victims of all serial killers, which is what we seem to be looking at here . . .'

'Seems so . . . agreed'

'Well, in all documented cases the victims tend to be women in young adulthood . . .'

'Yes . . . all right.'

'Because they go out at night . . . easy victims.'

'Yes,' Hennessey settled back in his chair, 'and they have their youthful attraction, and you are going to say those ladies do not fit that victim profile?'

'Yes, sir, that is what I am trying to say.' Webster held eye contact with Hennessey and then, deferentially, looked down. 'The first victim, or the last victim, but the first we identified, Miss Goodwin, she stands out as different from the others.'

'An anomaly?'

'Yes, sir, that's the very word. An anomaly.' He handed Hennessey a piece of paper. 'Going by height and date of disappearance, I believe these are the names of the victims in order of their age when they disappeared.'

Hennessey took the piece of paper from Webster. He read:

Angela Prebble, 33 years
Paula Rees, 39 years
Gladys Penta, 42 years
Rosemary Arkwright, 45 years
Helena Tunnicliffe, 51 years
Roslyn Farmfield, 57 years
Denise Clay, 63 years

'I see what you mean;' Hennessey spoke softly, 'the youngest is thirty-three years, the oldest sixty-three years, not at all the typical victim profile of serial killers of female victims.'

'There is one more victim, sir.'

'One more?'

'Yes, I can't fit her with any of our mis per reports but Dr D'Acre confirms she is, or was, middle-aged.'

'So we have nine victims, these seven, Veronica Goodwin and the as yet unidentified victim?'

'Yes, sir.'

'And, as you say, Veronica Goodwin at a tender twenty-three years is a distinct anomaly . . . but something will link them. They're all from the Vale? Yes, sorry, of course they are otherwise we wouldn't have their mis per files.'

'Yes, sir, just the one victim who might be foreign to the Vale, she is a short-term resident who had no social network, so no one to report her missing.'

'But eight out of the nine are definitely local to the Vale, they were left locally and in the same place . . . the perpetrator is local. The kitchen garden at Bromyards speaks loudly of local knowledge, no outsider here coming to the Vale to look for his victims, he knows this area . . . he's local.'

'Yes, sir.'

'And the victims, apart from the unidentified one, are local?'

'Furthest address from the city of York is at Shipton and that's only five miles away, a gentle stroll for a person in reasonable health, ten minutes by car and failing either, a frequent bus service.'

'Anything about the time sequence of their disappearances?'

'It seems there is a gap of between ten and twelve months between each disappearance. They all disappeared in the winter months.'

'Dark nights . . . poor visibility. Interesting. It could be a coincidence but I tend to think it isn't.'

'Yes, sir.'

'But it does mean that death came quickly to them . . . it suggests a quicker and more merciful death by hypothermia than the slower death by thirst that we were worried might be the case.'

'Yes . . . a small comfort.'

'Well, Yellich is gathering what information he can about the murder scene. Ventnor and Pharoah are interviewing people who knew Veronica Goodwin, so you and I will finish early for today. We'll review at nine tomorrow.'

'Yes, sir.'

'Have a restful night. I think we'll all be working hard for the foreseeable future.'

Reginald Webster, not at all displeased to be able to return home earlier than he had anticipated, drove to Selby via the quieter and more rural B1222 via Stillingfleet and Cawood. He turned into the housing estate in which he lived and announced his arrival by sounding his car horn twice, which he knew was, strictly speaking, a moving traffic offence, it being unlawful to sound a car's horn if (a) the car is stationary or (b) for any other purpose than to announce danger should the car be in motion. He was, however, known to his neighbours, all of whom knew and understood and approved of his method of announcing his arrival to his wife. As he parked his car the front door of his house opened and Joyce stood there smiling. He called a greeting to her, walked up the driveway and as he drew near he deliberately scuffed the gravel beside the concrete of the driveway. At the sound of the scuffed gravel his wife, blonde, short, slender, extended her arms. He embraced her and she responded instantly. Terry similarly greeted him by nudging his nose against his leg and wagging his tail.

That evening they sat down to a filling salad which had been lovingly prepared by Joyce, it being the only meal that he allowed her to prepare because hot food, and especially when created with boiling water, was too dangerous to risk. Later, as evening fell, Webster took Terry for a walk in the nearby woodland, because even working dogs need free time, and as he listened to a close by but unseen skylark he wondered at his wife's courage. Blinded at just twenty years of age when she was studying fine art at university and yet considering herself lucky because, of the four occupants in the car, she alone had survived.

George Hennessey did not do well in heat. He never understood why people would spend hard-earned money to bake in Corfu in July or August when they could visit Iceland instead, and leave it until January to visit the Mediterranean fleshpots when the weather there is bearable. He often said that if he were to be given a choice of Crete in August or Aberdeen in January, he would choose the latter without a moment's hesitation, it being preferable, in his mind, to keep warm in a cold climate rather than to try to keep cool in a hot climate. Because of his discomfort in heat he found sleep evaded him that evening. The hot day had given way to a warm evening and as he lay abed underneath just a single lightweight duvet with the window of his bedroom fully open, he still found it impossible to sleep. He was, though, at rest emotionally speaking and thinking of but not particularly preoccupied with the following day's tasks

. . . and then he heard the noise. Low at first but getting louder and louder and louder as it approached his house and then faded as the selfsame noise had once before faded into a similar summer's night. It was a motorbike. And at the sound his state of emotional rest erupted into turmoil.

The gap then appeared, the gap left by Graham, a void, huge, unmissable, a place which should have been filled by his elder brother who died in a motorbike accident when Hennessey was eight years old. An emptiness, always there . . .

George Hennessey's mind would not settle until the birds started to sing and the dawn began to appear, at which point sleep, wonderful, wonderful sleep came to him like a mother and took him unto her bosom.

It was 04.10 hours, Saturday, 13th June.

FOUR

Saturday, 13th June, 09.00 hours – 15.37 hours.
in which the core issue in the investigation becomes identified.

George Hennessey fought off the urge to sleep and smiled as he glanced round his team of officers assembled round his desk, each drinking tea from half-pint sized mugs patterned with many various logos and colours. Somerled Yellich, Carmen Pharoah, Thomson Ventnor and Reginald Webster, each looking refreshed and alert, and each clearly having benefited from a more solid and refreshing sleep than he had been able to manage until he was jarred into wakefulness at seven a.m. He similarly sipped a mug of hot tea, without which no Englishman can function and so which must be taken before the working day can commence. 'So,' Hennessey put his mug down gently on his desktop, 'we seem to have had a productive day yesterday, all busy . . . all got results . . . I have the overview, I read the recording before you filed it in here,' he patted the manila folder, marked just 'Bromyards Inquiry' but which was evidently thickening, 'but we need to share with each other. So, Somerled, as senior man, would you like to kick start us?'

'Yes, thank you, sir.' Yellich leaned forwards. 'I visited two people yesterday, both of whom know the house, Bromyards, very well. Both had very good things to say about Mr Housecarl, but perhaps the most useful information came from the elderly ex-head gardener, a chap called Sparrow, Jeff Sparrow, who told me that the kitchen garden at Bromyards could not, for the main part, be overlooked and that it was abandoned ten years ago, or so, about then, he couldn't give a certain date.'

'Yes,' Hennessey added, 'that fits in with the date of the abduction of the first victim . . .' he consulted the folder, 'one Angela Prebble, thirty-three years . . . after Veronica Goodwin's tender twenty-three years, she was the next youngest victim.'

'Yes, sir,' Yellich continued. 'Mr Sparrow also told me that the estate was well policed by poachers from the village. The estate, once it had been abandoned, appears to have been a major source of food for Milking Nook.' He smiled, 'I just love that name. I swear . . . only in England . . . but to continue, the estate was harvested by the locals for its game and fruit. They kept "alien" poachers from neighbouring villages out and kept a protective eye on Mr Housecarl, and didn't alarm him by letting off shotguns within a quarter of a mile of Bromyards. And yet . . . yet one or more persons was able to deposit nine bodies in the kitchen garden without being observed . . . but the quarter of a mile from the house is interesting because it explains why no one heard the women. They were gagged with rope ties, that would have prevented them from crying out for help, or from screaming, but they could have made a grunting sound and done so quite loudly, possibly loudly enough to carry for two hundred yards on a still night, especially in winter.'

'Yes,' Hennessey sipped his tea. 'Webster?'

'They all disappeared in the winter months,' Webster explained, 'well, eight did . . . the ninth body is as yet unidentified, but barring the possibility that they were kept against their will for up to six months, and if they were taken to Bromyards on the night of their abduction and left in the kitchen garden, then they would have died of hypothermia. They would have probably died before dawn. None had evidence of being clothed . . . no zip fasteners, or plastic buttons, or rotted remains of fabric.'

'So I thought I'd go back and talk to one of the poachers ... I am sure Jeff Sparrow could suggest a likely candidate. He or she could tell me what it would take to get a motor vehicle up to Bromyards without being seen.'

'Good idea,' Hennessey smiled. 'You've just talked your-self into a job.'

'Now,' Yellich continued, 'Mr Sparrow did once see a stranger on the estate, a person he described as a "townie". He gave a reasonable description but this was ten years ago.'

'So, at the time of the first disappearance?'

'Yes, sir. He apparently looked as though he was surveying the estate.'

'Him,' Hennessey pointed to Yellich, 'him we need to identify, if we can.'

'Yes, sir, if we can. Mr Sparrow also made a valid point, being that the man would have had to know the estate was there, the entrance to the drive isn't grand, it's modest, just the beginning of a driveway between two trees, no indica-tion that it's a mile long and leads to a mansion. You'd drive past it without noticing it. That man must have heard about Mr Housecarl abandoning his estate grounds, that information reached his ears by word of mouth. So he links, albeit vicariously, with someone in the village, whether an employee of Mr Housecarl's or not.'

'Yes,' again Hennessey smiled approvingly at Yellich, 'it's a link. Ensure you record that in the file.'

'Yes, sir.'

'Pharoah, Ventnor?'

'We looked into the first identified victim ... the last of the victims, Veronica Goodwin. I'm afraid we came up with a motiveless murder. Lived with her mother, employed at Gordon and Moxon's, on thin ice at work because of a drink problem, but we came across no one who would want to harm her and no reason for anyone to harm her. She seems to have been a random victim.'

'All right. So, Webster, back to you . . .'

'Well, the victims we might have identified, eight of the nine, make a strange picture . . . their ages are strange.' Webster glanced at his notes, 'Twenty-two years . . . thirty-three years . . . all right, that is the usual sort of age for a woman to fall victim to a serial killer but then the age of the victims rise up to sixty-three . . . highly unusual for female victims.'

'I'll say.' Yellich reclined in his chair.

'We need to find out more about the victims. Women of that age do not walk about the streets late at night; they are at home with their families.' Hennessey glanced out of the window of his office at the medieval walls of the city and noticed that they were beginning to crowd with tourists. 'They will link,' he said. 'Somewhere they will have something in common. So . . . Ventnor . . . you look at Angela Prebble and Paula Rees.'

'Yes, sir.'

'Pharoah.'

'Sir?'

'Gladys Penta and Rosemary Arkwright.'

'Yes, sir.'

'Webster . . . Helena Tunnicliffe and Roslyn Farmfield.'

'Yes, sir.'

'And you'd also better have Denise Clay as well.'

'Understood, sir.'

'Review here at nine tomorrow. Sunday working I know, but needs must.'

'Yes, sir.'

'For myself, I have a summons to see the Commander and then a press conference. I think I know what he wants.'

The man killed James Post by strangling him.

The man knew the other man was not up to it, not up to it at all, too weak, utterly spineless. So, when it was that James Post came running up the drive of the man's house, his face red with exertion, and panting so desperately that the man considered stepping back and letting the Post's heart do the job for him. But James Post calmed and sat on the man's couch, his face getting progressively paler as his breathing eased and he became a small man . . . worried . . . scared . . . a man who was childlike in his fear, so the other man, the householder, had always thought . . . and childlike in the absence of patience, childlike in his cruelty to his victims . . . to their victims. The householder had always scoffed at the notion of childhood innocence. Children, he had always argued, are psychopaths, damaging living things and each other with their absence of empathy. That is why scissors in primary schools are blunt with rounded ends, so that children do not stab each other. And here he is, he that can be so gleefully cruel, shaking with fear on the sofa, whimpering, 'What are we going to do? What are we going to do?' And so the second man, the calmer of the two, the householder, advanced on the whimpering man with his huge hands outstretched and calmly encircled the second man's neck with them and began to squeeze, and when James Post looked at him with terror in his eyes, the second man smiled at him and he continued smiling at him until James Post had stopped clawing at his hands and his body fallen limp. He carried James Post's body into his study and laid it on the floor and then drove into York looking for a suitable container. He found one in a charity shop. It was sufficiently large and robust, and he paid twice the asking price for it and left the shop with, 'Thank you, sir, very generous,' singing in his ears.

It was with no little reluctance that George Hennessey tapped on Commander Sharkey's door, and it was with no little reluctance that he accepted the invitation to sit in the chair in front of the Commander's desk.

'Things all right for you, George?' Sharkey asked warmly, but there was a nervousness in the warmth. 'I mean, I have no complaints about you but I am still worried. Not over-burdened?'

'No, sir, thank you all the same.'

'It's just that Johnny Taighe won't happen on my watch. It was a bad show. You know, I think about him more and more often. Our very able maths teacher left our school to advance himself and Johnny Taighe, who taught lower school maths, was told to teach final year maths to national certificate level. He just couldn't do it. He once froze in front of the blackboard because he couldn't understand the problem he'd put up, and he went and sat in a vacant seat next to a very able pupil and said, "What do you think we should do now?" That stays with me, George, a teacher leaving the front of the class to go and sit among the pupils because he couldn't understand the subject he was supposed to teach.'

'That is . . . unfortunate . . . yes, sir.'

'And he had a beer belly and a large, red nose, so he was drinking heavily . . . self-medicating with alcohol, and smoking too much . . . and was full of false good humour, all the indicators, and none of his colleagues picked up on them. He went home one night, complained of feeling unwell and had a massive coronary. That is not going to happen on my watch, so if things are getting too much for you, then let me know.'

'I am all right, sir,' Hennessey held up his hand. 'Thank you, but I am well on top of things now I have Pharoah, Webster and Ventnor to assist me, and Sergeant Yellich. I am more desk-bound than anything. I do miss front line policing though and go out when I can.'

'Yes, I have noticed . . . but you are sure you're on top of things?'

'Fully.'

'Good . . . well, like I said, I have no indications to the contrary but I want you to reach retirement. You don't have long to go, unlike me.' Sharkey smiled, he was fully ten

years Hennessey's junior. He was a short man, short for a
police officer, and an observer would perhaps see him as
being immaculately dressed. His desktop was, to
Hennessey's mind, always unhealthily neat and uncluttered,
very precise and with everything 'just so'. Sharkey would
not, thought Hennessey, be an easy man to live with. Behind
him, on the wall of his office, were two framed photographs, one showing a younger Sharkey in the uniform of
an officer in the British Army, and the other showing a
similar younger Sharkey in the uniform of an officer in the
Royal Hong Kong Police. 'The other thing, George . . . it
concerns me . . . is what I was part of when I wore that
uniform.' He half turned and indicated the photograph of
him in the Royal Hong Kong Police. 'I keep it there as a
kind of presence . . . this photograph,' he indicated the photograph of himself in the Army, 'this I am proud of . . . but
the Hong Kong experience. I was and remain contaminated.
It wasn't what you might call active corruption, it was of
a passive nature and I was only there for a brief period
of time but . . . I was told not to go into a certain area of
the city on a specific night and I did not, I took my patrol
elsewhere and the following morning there would be a brown
paper envelope full of cash in my desk drawer. That's just
the way it was. If I had blown the whistle or taken my
patrol where I was told not to take it, I would have had my
throat cut, I'd disappear, be found floating in the harbour.
I got out when I could but I couldn't cope with anything
like that here in Micklegate Bar. You must tell me if there
is a whiff of anything like that.'

'Yes, sir, I will . . . you have my word.'

'Thank you, George. Thank you.'

The man eyed Yellich with what seemed to Yellich to be
an expression of approval and appreciation and also a degree
of recognition of a kindred spirit. 'You're a hunter,' he said.

Yellich smiled. 'A hunter? Confess I have been called

many things in my life but a hunter, that's a new one. Why do you say that?'

'It's in your eyes . . . looking, constantly looking . . . left to right . . . noticing but you stand still.'

Yellich pursed his lips. 'I'll be careful not to give myself away.'

'You can't hide it, not from someone that can recognize it.'

The man stood in his front garden, spade in hand. He was of a lean, sinewy build. He wore baggy gardening trousers and he had rolled his shirtsleeves up to his elbows. His head was shielded from the sun with a white wide-brimmed canvas cricketer's hat. Beyond the man's garden was a field of ripening wheat and beyond that a small stand of trees, and then began the undulating grass covered hills of the Yorkshire Wolds, all beneath a vast canopy of blue, scarred at that moment with the vapour trail of an airliner flying high over England from Continental Europe to North America, within which, thought Yellich, the passengers in the window seats would be looking down on a panorama of England. 'So, they told you where to find me at the pub?' He glanced questioningly at his watch.

'The publican told me. He was outside the pub stacking empty beer kegs. I assured him that I was making inquiries re the dead bodies found at Bromyards and I only wanted information about poaching on the estate. I told him I wouldn't be getting anybody charged. We're looking for a felon, or felons, who murdered nine women; we are not bothered about a pheasant or two being taken, especially if we haven't received a complaint from the landowner.'

'Fair enough.'

'The publican said that you hadn't done it for a long time and you might have given up the game, but he said that you'd be the man to ask.'

'Charlie? Yes, he's good like that but I haven't retired . . . no poacher ever retires, just stop when they have to but they

never decide to stop. If their health fails they'll stop . . .
if they get gaoled they'll stop. So, anyway, how can I help
you?'

'Well, it's simply this, Dick,' Yellich said. 'You don't
mind if I call you Dick?'

'No . . . Dick is fine,' Dick Fallon replied, wiping a bead
of sweat from his brow. Yellich thought that he also had
hunter's eyes, searching, searching and missing little. He
drove the spade into the soil and rested one hand upon
the handle.

'We have spoken to a few people and they told us that
the poachers on the Bromyards estate kept an eye on Mr
Housecarl.'

'Yes . . . yes, that's a fair thing to say. He was very good
to the village . . . he'll be missed.'

'So we understand. So, the question is, what difficulty
would a man or men have in getting a body on to the estate,
from the public highway right up to Bromyards and
depositing it in the kitchen garden, and do that about once
a year for about ten years?'

'Ten bodies?'

'Nine . . .'

Dick Fallon glanced at the soil he had turned, creating
neat lines of deep trenches in the ground, opening it in good
time to let the first of the frost in, when autumn arrives.
'That is a question because not a lot goes unseen here. Like
all villages, you can walk for miles without seeing anybody,
but you can put good money on the chance that someone
will have their eyes on you at any one time.' Fallon looked
around him. 'Bad weather would be a good time . . . less
game about in the winter; the trout pond will have frozen
over . . .'

'Good point.'

'But poachers set snares and will go and check on them
all year round.'

'Yes, but less so in the winter?'

'Yes . . . and a rainy, stormy night, that sort of weather keeps the game well down and the poachers well at home.'

'That's a good point. Weekends or weekday?'

'Weekday . . . too many of the village children exploring the grounds at weekends, especially in the summer, but they wouldn't go near the house for fear of disturbing Mr Housecarl, they were very well warned about that.'

'I see,' Yellich nodded, 'that is another good point.'

'He or they wouldn't go near the estate in the snow.'

'You think not?'

'I think not. They'd leave tracks and there'd be the danger of getting stuck in a snow drift. The drive is a mile long and not kept clear of snow.'

'Again . . . useful.' Yellich's eye was caught by a yellow-hammer which alighted a nearby fence post, one of a number of black pitch pointed staves which separated Dick Fallon's garden from the adjacent field. He had not seen an example of that species in many, many years and the sight of a relatively rare bird uplifted his spirits.

'You know, if I were up to no good I'd go on the estate in the forenoon come to think of it.'

'Really?'

'Yes, poachers don't like staying out all night; they like to go to bed . . . some have jobs to go to. If they don't, they'll sleep late. So about seven, eight, nine a.m. that would be a good time to drive on to the estate with headlights off and dump a body in the kitchen garden and drive away again, and if the rain was really siling down and the wind was blowing it sideways then, that would be a very good time to do it with little risk of being seen, and if you didn't drive through the village, if you approached from the south and left by the south, you wouldn't have to go through Milking Nook.'

'This has been very useful.'

'I'll put the word round the village. If anyone knows anything, they'll contact you.'

'A tall, well-built man was seen, a "townie". Could be unconnected but we'd like to trace him, though it was about ten years ago that he was seen on the estate . . .'

Fallon smiled a wry knowing smile, 'About when it all started, like he was checking the place out? I'll say you want to talk to him . . . but, yes . . . tall, well-built townie. I'll put the word out for you about him as well, though it's probably out already if you've talked to other villagers, but I'll mention it this lunchtime. I take lunch at the pub you see.'

Crestfallen. It was the only word Ventnor could think of to describe David Prebble. He seemed utterly crestfallen. 'I did wonder, you couldn't help but wonder.' Prebble looked down at the ground and seemed unable to take his gaze anywhere else. Ventnor saw him as a short, sturdy man with receding grey hair and who was casually dressed in khaki shorts, leather sandals and a white tee shirt with, somewhat incongruously, Ventnor thought, 'Hawaii' emblazoned upon it in eye-catching blue. He seemed to Ventnor to dress like Ventnor did when off duty, sleepily grabbing the first clean item of clothing which came to hand each morning and caring nothing about the image he presented. 'You'd better come in, sir.' He stepped aside to allow Ventnor to enter his house. Ventnor found the interior of Prebble's house to be untidy and poorly ventilated and as such, having a musty smell. Ventnor counted three flies buzzing against the window pane and saw a further two contentedly walking across the glass. 'See me,' Prebble smiled meekly, 'I'm just not the best housekeeper in the world.' He spoke with a distinct Scottish accent of the Western Isles, softer than the harsh sounding accent of Scotland's Central Belt. 'I let things go a wee bit after Angela disappeared and,' he indicated the room, 'this is tidy, sir. I mean, I keep things clean, as clean as I can, but I let things lie where I drop them. I know where everything is though. I mean, see that pile of clothes there?' Prebble pointed to a collection of outer garments which occupied an armchair. 'In that lot, about halfway down is a pair of binoculars. I haven't used them since spring time two years ago when I took them to the Dales to look for the peregrine falcon that was reported to be there, and they'll stay there until I need them again. My wallet's in my other pair of shorts. This is how I live but our Angie, she couldn't bear anything out of place. Fussy she was and I did wonder if she was one of the women that had been found. Milking Nook . . . what a name for a village, eh?'

'You are Mr Prebble?' Ventnor spoke firmly. 'I'm sorry but I have to be certain as to whom I am talking.'

'Yes, sir.' Prebble answered promptly, sharply, deferentially. He was significantly older than Ventnor. 'David, "Davy", Prebble . . . railwayman all my days, ticket office clerk. It pays our . . . my, it pays my mortgage. As you see, the house is no fancy mansion.'

'It's very cosy,' Ventnor smiled. It was, he thought, a fair description of the Prebble household, at the back of the railway station, clearly conveniently close to Davy Prebble's place of work. 'These are solid houses. There's a lot to be said for houses of this vintage. I would not buy a modern house . . . nothing later than 1939 for me. I have an inter-war house.'

'Good for you, sir. As you say, solidly built, it did me and Angie all right.'

'Good. So . . . I read the missing persons report on Angela. You are . . . you were Mr and Mrs Prebble?'

'No, sir. We were Mr and Miss Prebble, brother and sister. We used to live in a small town, a village really on the Isle of Lewis, it was very Free Church of Scotland, which is really anything but free in its attitude . . . Sabbath observation, no alcohol on Sundays, all amusement is sinful and then when our Angie fell pregnant to a local boy . . . well, the shame was too much for her to bear, so she allowed the bairn to be put up for adoption and she grew to regret that decision so she did, and she especially regretted it after moving to England where folk don't think the same . . . not having a wedded parent is not seen as being so bad.'

'No, it's not shameful at all,' Ventnor agreed, 'not any more at least.'

'So, well, I'd been out . . . out of the "Wee Free's" influence. I joined the RAF and did three years with them, just the minimum service . . . the air force regiment . . . guarding air fields with my rifle and Alsatian, but it did what I wanted it to do, it freed me from the "Free's", it got me out of Stornoway, got me away from all that attitude. So, when Angie said she couldn't go to the Kirk and be made to stand up in front of the congregation to be named along with all the other fallen women of the town and so was going to leave the island, I said I'd go with her. We pooled our money together, so we did, and worked out how far we could get to, and the answer was York. That was twenty years ago, about that sort of time. We rented accommodation and then got jobs, got a mortgage on this wee house and we moved in and let the neighbours think we were man and wife, until they got to be friends and then we told them the truth, but emphasized we had separate rooms. There was nothing like that going on, sir, not ever, nothing untoward at all.'

'All right . . . all right.'

'Well, do sit down if you can find a space,' Dave Prebble said with a sheepish smile, 'it's all clean. Untidy, yes, but clean. I scrub the bath and toilet and change the bed linen each week, and take clothes to the launderette each week, but things sort of stay where I drop them.'

Ventnor mumbled his thanks and sat on the settee next to a pile of railway enthusiast magazines.

'So, she has been found,' Prebble lowered himself on to a pile of clothing and settled as if perched on them, working his way into them until he was comfortable. 'Her body has been found?'

'Possibly. We still have to confirm the identity.'

'I understand, but it's going to be her. We were very close and I knew harm had come to her when she didn't return home. She had no reason to run away . . . she had no one to go to. She pined for the bairn but she hated Stornoway and she wouldn't return there. I walked the streets looking for her. I knew I wouldn't find her but I couldn't stay at home . . . those long nights, then they became weeks, then months . . . then years, nearly ten years. I accepted the inevitable a long time ago and realized the only reason the police would call on me was if she had been found.'

'Well, as I say, there is no definite match but a woman . . . the remains of a woman, who was Angela's height and age at the time of Angela's disappearance is one of the remains you have heard about.'

'Yes . . . I did wonder, as I told you. How can I help you?'

'With her positive identification. A full-face photograph, anything with her DNA on it . . . failing that, anything with your DNA will do.'

'DNA. Yes, I heard about that, better at eliminating than proving, I believe?'

'Yes. British courts cannot convict on DNA evidence alone, but as you say, it's useful for eliminating suspects and very useful for establishing identities, as in this case.'

'I see. I don't think I have a photograph you can use; we didn't photograph each other as a married couple might. We holidayed separately which is when you'd likely take photographs of each other.'

'All right, but we'll need something of hers.'

'I'll see what's in her room.'

'So what can you tell me about your sister which you think might be relevant to her disappearance?'

'Glad you added that bit at the end,' Prebble grinned, 'because I can tell you a lot about her.'

'Yes, imagine you can,' Ventnor smiled. 'Did she have any enemies, for instance?'

Prebble teetered back on the pile of clothes. 'No, I don't think she did. I think it's safe for me to say that. She had folk she didn't like ... like all those petty minded Wee Free's at home. She hated the social worker who persuaded her to give up the bairn for adoption when she should have supported her and encouraged her to keep it, and that was before it was born ... so he was taken from her immediately. She didn't even get to hold him, not even for a few seconds, that "holier than thou" bitch, Angela hated her, but she wasn't even sixteen at the time, she was little more than a child herself. He'll be a man in his twenties now. We don't even know what his Christian name is. So she had a lot of bad feelings for all that crew up there, but I know of no one who'd want to harm her.'

'Fair enough. What did your sister do for a living?'

'Nursery nurse, she worked in a nursery, next best thing to having her own child I suppose.'

'Which nursery was that?'

'St Urban's "First Steps" nursery ... it's still there, attached to St Urban's Primary School in Escrick, all part of the St Urban's experience. Start at eighteen months, or two years, or three years, go right through to eighteen and leave to attend university. Roman Catholic foundation, a very good school; leave full of Catholic guilt, so they say, but they get excellent results ... so they say.'

'I see.'

'Well, Angie was down the soft end before they start filling them with the notion of sin and eternal damnation. She was all cuddly toys and beginning of speech ... toilet training. Paid badly but she was content and we survived.'

'Did she have any friends?'

'A few ... colleagues mostly, but by and large we kept to ourselves.'

'Understood. So what was she like as a person?'

'Angie?' Davy Prebble inclined his head to one side. 'I'd

describe her as quiet. She would go out occasionally but was always home by nine p.m.'

'Did she meet up with her colleagues in the evening? That is on those evenings that she did go out?'

'I can't tell you, sir, I didn't pry. She just said she had been with "friends".'

'OK . . . but you wouldn't know the names of any of her friends?' Ventnor pressed Prebble.

'Just one, as I recall, she mentioned him once or twice, a guy by the name of Ronald Malpass.'

Ventnor wrote 'Malpass, Ronald', in his notebook.

'Aye, Ronald, our Angie seemed fair fond of him so she did, fair fond . . . had a lot of time for him.'

'Do you know of his address?'

'Yes . . .' Davy Prebble's eyes brightened and he held up his index finger. 'Yes, I do . . . excuse me.' He slid off the pile of clothes and left the room returning a few moments later with a handful of letters. He held them up triumphantly. 'This is the mail that Angie received after she went missing. I kept them all, not many, but I kept them all. After a while all that was addressed to her was junk mail, which I put in the bin, but these came for her. So, she disappeared in late November of that year and she got these Christmas cards and one of them,' he looked on the reverse of each card, 'one of them . . . yes, this one . . . has the sender's address on the back of the envelope, in the continental style of doing things. Here you are . . .'

                    Ronald Malpass
                    2 Portland Street
                    Hutton Cranswick

He handed the envelope to Ventnor who copied the address into his notebook.

'That's quite a journey, Hutton Cranswick, it's out by Driffield. Quite a well to do little place by all accounts but

I have never actually been there; it was Angie who told me it was a well to do wee place.'

Ventnor looked at the postmark and saw the envelope had been posted on the fifteenth of December that year. 'Would you mind if I opened this envelope?'

Prebble looked uncomfortable. 'Frankly, I would. Can you wait until her identity is confirmed? If it is then you can open and read all the letters.'

'That's fair. I'll need something with her DNA or a swab of your DNA.'

'Her hairbrush, how about that? It has some of her hair in the bristles.'

'Ideal,' Ventnor smiled. 'Ideal.'

The man and woman sat side by side on the settee looking at the television and as they watched George Hennessey rise and leave the press conference the woman turned to the man and smiled. 'You have made quite a splash, darling.'

'We,' the man squeezed her hand gently, 'we have made quite a splash. It's international news, apparently.'

'Yes . . . the yellow helicopter hovering over York . . . it's not the police helicopter . . . it must belong to a television news company, taking footage of York and out to Bromyards . . . especially Bromyards. It looks quaint from the air . . . they both do.'

'As you say . . . quaint. But soon it will be time.'

'Yes, darling . . . I know.'

'Gladys,' the man sighed deeply. 'It's been six or seven years . . . possibly more, I have lost count.' He dropped the sponge into the red plastic bucket of warm soapy water and turned away from the car he was cleaning. 'I'm not really supposed to do this,' he nodded at the car, 'water's getting short.'

'I know,' Carmen Pharoah replied in a solemn tone of voice.

'Well, there's no hosepipe ban yet and, as you see, I use a bucket of water, but I need something to do. Even now I still need something to do, I get a bit lost without her . . . but I use the bath water to water the garden, so I am economizing.'

'Good for you.'

'Well let's talk inside . . .'

The interior of Martyn Penta's house was, Carmen Pharoah observed, neat, and clean and tidy. 'The maids have just been in,' he explained.

'The maids?'

'A team of cleaning women, young women really, plus one man-maid, help me keep on top of the house. I could not manage it on my own, heavens no.'

Carmen Pharoah smiled. The interior of the house did indeed smell strongly of cleaning liquids and air freshener. 'I see.'

'Well, do take a pew.'

Carmen Pharoah settled on to the deeply upholstered and wide leather-bound settee and read affluence in the room, but this was after all Heslington, and Martyn Penta was, after all, an accountant. 'You are not working today, Mr Penta?'

'Yes, I am, I'm working at home. I do that usually unless I have clients to interview. I very rarely go into the office these days courtesy of IT and the web. I can do everything in my study upstairs that I can in my office in York. Any documents I need can be faxed to me and I can send by fax, but I was in a putting-off-work frame of mind today so I washed the car as an excuse not to go up to my study . . . then I got your phone call about Gladys. So I carried on washing the car until you arrived . . . and here you are.'

'Yes, sir, here I am.'

'She hated that name.'

'Gladys?'

'Yes, she said it made her sound Edwardian.' Martyn

Penta smiled as if recovering a pleasant memory. Carmen Pharoah observed him to be a well-set man in his middle years, clean-shaven and wearing expensive looking casual clothes, even to wash the car. 'It made her sound as old as her great aunt after whom she was named, so she said, and did she hate it, but she wouldn't change it out of a sense of loyalty to her parents . . . So what news do you have?'

'We believe she might have been found.'

'Alive!'

'Sadly, no, I do regret to say.'

'Well, it was too much to hope but you do read of such things, someone suddenly losing their memory and is committed to an institution, and then banging their head and remembering everything.'

'Stuff of fiction, I'm afraid.'

'Yes, these days of records and files which follow you around, not so easy as it was for the Victorians who could stage their suicide and disappear, and reinvent themselves with a new name in another city . . . usually having emptied the bank account just beforehand.'

'You sound disappointed.'

'That's probably because I am disappointed, disappearing and reinventing myself somewhere else is a fantasy I have long harboured. So, tell me what you have come to tell me.'

Carmen Pharoah told Martyn Penta of the possible inclusion of his late wife's remains among the human remains found at Bromyards. He fell silent and Carmen Pharoah allowed him a few moments of 'space' before she asked what he recalled about his wife's disappearance.

'Like it was yesterday. I was away when she vanished. I was attending a conference on the Isle of Man. She wasn't at home when I returned from the conference but seems to have been missing for about three days, going by the accumulation of mail in the letterbox. I reported her missing the following day, after phoning all her relatives and all our friends.'

'Did you have any idea where she might have gone?'

'The only place she went to at all were those wretched meetings.'

'The meetings?'

'It was . . . they were the only thing she lived for. I loved my wife, I will cherish her memory, but she was a six-cylinder, supercharged, dyed in the wool alcoholic. She was a dry alcoholic; she hadn't touched a drink for years before she vanished but, as she was fond of saying, once an alcoholic, always an alcoholic. She had replaced one addiction with another, "Hello, I am Gladys and I am alcoholic". "Hello, Gladys" they would all reply. I went to a few meetings with her you see, she became a "personality" within AA, a guest speaker at the various meetings in this region telling folk how she used to drink two bottles of gin each day . . . which she did . . . up at eight, already drunk by ten a.m., and now she was "free" and the meeting would applaud her, that's when I stopped going.'

'Oh.'

'Attention seeking and replacing one addiction with another. She had got on top of the booze but became obsessed with AA and had little time for me or our marriage. AA was utterly central to her life and I was on the edge. I also found out that Alcoholics Anonymous has a perverted sense of snobbery. I mean, if you get up and say you used to drink beer and only beer nobody would talk to you, even though it might have cost you your job and marriage just as whisky might have, but they were interested in you if you were into spirits or the cheap wine, and they were in awe of Gladys's two bottle a day habit but she could be knocked off her perch if a three bottles a day person joined the meeting.'

'That's quite illuminating.'

'I had my eyes opened all right . . . but she was never home, it was one group in the mornings, another in the afternoon and another in the evenings. I was not even second fiddle to the AA. I was in her life in name only. But I still miss her dreadfully.'

'I'm sorry. What we really have to do is to confirm her identity . . . dental records or a sample of her DNA.'

'Yes . . . she had a climbing accident when she was a young woman; the left side of her face was permanently concave. She was very self-conscious about it; it was then that she started drinking . . . distinct injury to her skull. She was lucky to have survived and luckier still to have escaped serious brain damage.'

'As you say . . . that might be sufficient to confirm her identity but what you report about her drink problem might be very significant.'

'You think so?'

'Yes,' Carmen Pharoah stood, 'I think so. I really think so.'

Thomson Ventnor drove back to Micklegate Bar Police Station, signed in, and went directly to the office of DCI Hennessey. He tapped on the door frame, entered the office and sat, uninvited, in one of the chairs in front of Hennessey's desk. 'I am mindful of your previous admonition, boss,' he explained smiling.

'Oh?' Hennessey put his pen down and reclined in his chair. 'Which particular admonition was that?'

'Charging off without clearing it with you, sir, even though I had my mobile phone with me,' he tapped his jacket pocket.

'Yes, I remember, I am so pleased that you took that issue on board, it is essential that I keep the overview and also it is essential that I know where each of my team is, at all times.'

'Yes, sir.'

'So, do I assume . . . may I assume there is a development?'

'Just another possible contact about one of the victims, Angela Prebble . . . she is a Miss Prebble, not Mrs, and the man she shared her house with is her brother, not her husband.'

'Ah . . . I see.'

'He made reference to her friends but despite that, he painted a picture of a very socially isolated pair of individuals. One friend of hers sent a Christmas card with his name and address on the reverse of the envelope. I feel that he, the friend, might be more in the loop . . . in Miss Prebble's loop than is, or was, her own brother, but I was only briefed to interview the next of kin. I am happy to go and see him alone but I thought I'd better clear it with yourself first, sir, and also do a criminal records check.'

'Yes, thank you. I am pleased you did that, but it sounds like a two-hander.' Hennessey reached for his phone and, lifting the receiver, he pressed a four figure internal number. 'Criminal records?' he asked when his call was answered. 'Good . . .' he glanced at Ventnor questioningly.

Ventnor responded, 'Ronald Malpass, Two Portland Street, Hutton Cranswick.'

Hennessey repeated the name and address and then looked at Ventnor a second time.

Ventnor shook his head and said, 'No numbers, sir.'

'No date of birth,' Hennessey added, as he heard the sound of a computer keyboard being tapped rapidly and efficiently. Then he said, 'All right, thank you.' He replaced the phone gently. 'No major crime . . . just a few for drunk and disorderly, and one drunk in charge of a motor vehicle . . . all dealt with by the magistrates and some time ago . . . all spent convictions now, but I still think I'd like you to take someone with you.'

'As you wish, sir.'

'Contact Carmen Pharoah. Ask her to meet you at the address.'

'Yes, sir.'

The man who had murdered James Post and his wife sat in silence in the living room of their home. The brains of both were active but there was just nothing to say once the man had said, 'No point in burying . . . not now.'

Carmen Pharoah followed Martyn Penta to the door of his house when the mobile phone vibrated in her handbag and played the 'William Tell Overture'. 'Excuse me.' She halted and plunged her hand into her handbag.

'Of course, and may I compliment you on your choice of ringtone? So many ringtones are for the brain dead.'

Carmen Pharoah smiled at the compliment and then, holding the device to her right ear, said, 'Hello, Thompson.' She fell silent before replying, 'I'll see you there. I am just leaving Mr Penta's house now, I'll see you there. I'll look for your car.' She smiled at Martyn Penta as she slid her mobile phone into her handbag. 'Day in the life of a copper, one thing after the other.'

Martyn Penta opened the door of his house to allow her to egress the building. 'Well, it's better than being out of work and thanks, you've jolted me into a sense of urgency in respect of my work. I have balance sheets to address.'

In the event, it was Thomson Ventnor who identified Carmen Pharoah's car and he halted behind it. He left his own car, walked to hers and sat in the front passenger seat. 'Sorry, I took the wrong turning.'

'I've only just got here myself.' Carmen Pharoah gazed at the line of detached houses reaching away from her on the right-hand side, to the left was a large village green complete with duck pond and war memorial, beyond which stood a row of prestigious looking houses which seemed to represent the 'posh' side of the village green. 'The address is just up there and round the corner. I enquired at the post office which I found inside the general store. It's that sort of village.' She started the engine of her car. 'Following me or leaving yours here?'

'Leaving it,' Ventnor pulled the seat-belt across his chest, 'pick it up on the way back. This fella has some previous I should tell you, all minor, drink related, all spent.'

'Drink again?'

'Yes, may not be anything but alcohol related. Demon drink is getting to be a bit of a common theme.'

'It is, isn't it?' Ventnor glanced at the war memorial as they drove past it. 'Veronica Goodwin . . .'

'And Gladys Penta. I have just visited her husband. She was the cornerstone of the local chapter of Alcoholics Anonymous.'

'That is interesting.'

Carmen Pharoah smiled. 'That's exactly what I said.'

'Well it at least makes a change.' Hennessey smiled as he made the remark. 'In fact, I think it's a first.'

'It's a new one on me also, sir.' The uniformed sergeant of the police was, thought Hennessey, clearly of sufficient years' service to be able to say that. 'Usually it's dog walkers or children'.

'Or courting couples.' Hennessey strode across the baked, hard ground, side by side with the sergeant, towards the small stand of trees by which stood a white inflatable tent, the location being cordoned off by a line of blue and white police tape. 'That's happened before, a young couple seeking some privacy, entering a secluded area and lo' and behold, a dead body . . . rather putting a damper on any romantic notion they might have been entertaining.'

'I'll say,' the uniformed sergeant replied drily, and without any trace of humour. Hennessey had not met the man before and sensed he was in the company of a bitter man who probably felt he should have achieved a higher rank than he had achieved, and who was approaching his retirement from a modest station.

The police constable at the tape inclined his head in acknowledgement of Hennessey and the sergeant and lifted the tape to allow them to enter the restricted area. The interior of the wooded area was pleasantly shaded but unpleasantly, Hennessey thought, contaminated by the buzzing of a large swarm of flies. Hennessey entered the inflatable tent which stood beside the trees. Dr Mann was already present.

'Adult male,' Dr Mann announced, 'adult of the male sex. I have confirmed life extinct at fourteen twenty hours, about twenty-five minutes ago.'

'I see. Thank you.'

'I have contacted York District Hospital and requested the attendance of a forensic pathologist.'

'Understood . . . and again, thank you.' Hennessey looked at the body. 'The commander won't like me being here, he has me desk-bound these days out of concern for my health, but all my team are committed so it's all hands to the pump.' He saw the remains, recent remains of a small man, with a pinched and pointed face of the type that often makes appearances before magistrates, and often does so with an air of resentment and indignation that his day has been interrupted for the purpose. Hennessey thought the man had almost ferret-like features. He wore tight-fitting clothing with pointy-toed shoes upon his feet. Hennessey had met the type before, not punching other people but, once the victim had been knocked to the ground, he would wade in, kicking with his pointy-toed shoes and doing considerable damage thereby. 'Winkle-pickers.'

'Sorry, sir?' Dr Man smiled.

'These shoes, they were fashionable when I left the navy in the 1950s, used to be called "winkle-pickers". I didn't know they were still available and worn by the likes of him. He doesn't look like he could have put up any kind of fight but he wears that sort of shoe, a man in need of victims methinks.'

'Yes, sir.'

'His age, what do you think?'

'Middle years,' Dr Mann replied. 'Fifties perhaps, he could even be older.'

'Yes, closer to drawing his state pension than his embittered teenage years, yet still in his teens in his head. I mean, those shoes at that sort of age. Suspicious death though.'

'Very,' Dr Mann replied softly, 'the bruising round his neck, can't miss it.'

'Can't, can you? How long do you think he's been here?'

'That's one for the pathologist but, I'd say he was killed within the last forty-eight hours . . . probably twenty-four if no attempt has been made to chill his body,' the slender turbaned police surgeon replied. 'But I can't be drawn, it is not my place.'

'Neither will the forensic pathologist,' Hennessey replied with a grin. He turned to the elderly sergeant. 'Any identification?'

'None sir, unless it's well hidden in his clothing . . . no wallet that we can find, although we did find his library card.'

'That might do it.'

'It's been bagged and tagged, sir . . . local library with a valid date.'

'Well if it is his card, we have his ID.'

'Yes, sir.'

'So, he was not a wealthy man.' Hennessey pondered the corpse, cheap, inexpensive clothing and watch. 'So, not murdered for his money but his wallet, if he had one, was taken, so it must have been taken to frustrate his being identified, but the killer missed the library card. So, in a hurry or just carelessly assuming that his wallet contained all that could identify him.'

'Forensic pathologist has arrived, sir,' the young constable at the tape announced in a keen, eager to help manner.

Hennessey turned and felt his heart leap in his chest as he watched the slender figure of Dr D'Acre approach carrying a heavy Gladstone bag. 'Take her bag for her,' he asked of the constable, who instantly ran towards Dr D'Acre and relieved her of her burden. He walked half a pace behind her until she reached the tape, upon which he stepped forward and lifted it for her. She smiled her thanks and retook possession of her bag.

Dr D'Acre glanced at the corpse and then gently set her Gladstone bag down upon the ground and opened it. She disturbed the clothing to take a rectal temperature and then a ground temperature. Stony-faced she glanced up at DCI Hennessey and said, 'I know what you are going to ask, Chief Inspector, and you know what the answer is.'

'Yes, ma'am,' Hennessey smiled. 'I have learned my lesson, made my journey . . . between the time he was last seen alive and the time the body was discovered is as close as medical science can get.'

'Except possibly in this case . . . maggot pupae are in evidence. I'll take one or two samples, but their presence means he died some time within the last forty-eight hours . . . but this heat,' she brushed flies from her face, 'it could speed things. Rigor is established and you can see for yourself that as corpses go, this is quite a fresh corpse.' She paused. 'I note bruising round the neck.'

'Yes, ma'am, Dr Mann mentioned those marks.'

'Could not fail to notice them . . . extensive . . . not linear, suggestive of manual strangulation. If he had been garrotted with rope, or a length of electrical flex, then we would expect linear bruising, but this is extensive . . . and . . .' she felt the scalp of the deceased, 'a possible skull fracture. Possibly rendered unconscious with strangulation and then he sustained a massive blow to the head to finish him off. I see no sign of a struggle hereabouts, so he was most likely conveyed here possibly within a container, such as a cabin trunk, and deposited where he was found. Definitely murder and within the last forty-eight hours, with a time window of twelve hours either side of that.'

'Understood and appreciated. It is at least something to go on.'

Dr D'Acre stood. 'Well, if you have taken all the photo-graphs you need to take, then from my point of view the body can be taken to York District Hospital for the post-mortem.'

'SOCO?' Hennessey turned to the uniformed sergeant.

'Still to arrive, sir.'

Hennessey glanced skywards in a gesture of despair, and noted a single wispy cloud in the canopy of blue. 'We should bring them with us, then they won't keep getting lost all the time.'

'Yes, sir.'

'Contact them, if you can, hurry them along. We need their cameras here asap.'

The uniformed sergeant gripped the radio on his lapel and pressed the send button, and walked towards the centre of the field as he did so, presumably, thought Hennessey, that he might achieve a better reception.

'I presume you are going to remove the scalp?' Hennessey turned to Dr D'Acre who, dressed in white coveralls in such bright sunshine, caused Hennessey to squint when looking at her.

'I'll have to,' Dr D'Acre replied matter-of-factly, 'head injuries. I'll have to look at it. Why do you ask?'

'It will aid identification if you can delay doing the post-mortem.'

'I see. Yes, I can delay doing it.'

'We have what might be his library card. If it is his, it will give us his address, then we can get a next of kin to view the corpse.'

'Never easy, but yes, I can delay to allow that. Doesn't sound like you'll need a great deal of time?'

'I anticipate it being done today.'

'Will you be observing for the police, Chief Inspector?'

'Yes, I will.'

'Very good. I'll return to York District, I have a post-mortem still to conduct . . . university student.'

'Oh . . . narcotics overdose?'

'Don't believe so, not alcohol either. Found lying in his bed with very blue lips, indication of carbon monoxide poisoning, probably caused by a faulty flue on his gas fire.'

'He had his gas fire on in this weather?'

'He was Malaysian; even this weather is cold for them.'

'I see.'

'So, how was he discovered?' Dr D'Acre pointed to the body on the ground covered with the tent.

'By a swarm of flies.'

'A swarm of flies?' she grinned at Hennessey.

'A sharp-eyed lady in those houses over there . . .' Hennessey pointed to a line of houses on the far side of the field, the ground floors of which were hidden from view. 'She glanced out of her bedroom window and saw the column of black flies beside the trees. She knew the field is not being used for pastoral grazing at the moment and knew that flies in such numbers are attracted to newly deceased animals or humans, so she strolled across the field and . . . here we are.'

'New one on me, it's usually dog walkers or courting couples.'

George Hennessey smiled gently, 'Yes, it is, isn't it?'

The middle-aged, smartly dressed man stood facing the heavy velvet curtain. He was a small man, so short in stature that Hennessey, standing beside him, felt that he was towering over the man. The room was dark, being dimly lit, heavily carpeted with darkly stained, heavily polished wood panelling on the walls. The man took a deep breath as he and Hennessey waited for the nurse.

'It won't be like what you . . .'

'I know,' the man turned to Hennessey and forced a smile, 'I have done this before.'

'Really? I am sorry.'

'My wife, she was knocked down and killed by a drunken driver and I had to identify the body. As you say, it's not like it's portrayed in the films, lifting a sheet over a body that is in a metal drawer . . . more sensitive . . . the last image I had of my wife was of her sleeping in space.'

At that moment, the smaller of the two doors to the room opened, silently, and a sombre looking nurse entered. She glanced at Hennessey who gave a single slight nod of his head. The nurse then pulled a cord and the velvet curtains slid open, again silently. What was revealed to Hennessey and the man was a pane of glass, and beyond the glass was the body of the man who had been found earlier that day when a householder had noticed a swarm of flies. The body was, by then, tightly swathed in clean white bandages with only the facial features showing. Nothing else could be discerned, just an endless seeming blackness. It was as the man had described, as if the person on the bed was at peace, floating in deep space.

'Yes,' the man spoke quietly, 'yes, that is James, James Post, my younger brother.'

'Thank you, and I am sorry.' He once again nodded to the nurse who pulled another cord and shut the curtains. 'Can you answer some questions?'

'Here?'

'No, we'll go to the interview suite at the police station.'

Hennessey drove Mr Nigel Post, brother of James, to Micklegate Bar Police Station. The journey was passed in silence.

In the interview suite, Nigel Post settled into the chair and glanced round the room at the orange coloured walls and the hard-wearing carpet of similar colour, though of a darker shade of the same. 'Not as functional as I imagined,' he commented.

'We have more functional rooms for interviewing suspects,' Hennessey replied, 'upright chairs, table, tape recorders set in the wall, but for less formal Q and As we use this room.' He sat opposite Nigel Post and rested his notebook on his lap.

'If you could tell me about your brother?'

Post reclined back in the chair and eyed Hennessey with a look of concern. 'You would only bring me here and ask that question if there was some suspicion about his death. When my wife was killed by that idiot I was only asked to identify her body.'

'Yes . . .' Hennessey avoided eye contact with Nigel Post, 'I am afraid that this is a murder inquiry.'

Post leaned forward. 'What happened?'

'We don't know. Yet. The post-mortem has still to be conducted but injuries were noticed on your brother's body about his neck and head, and he was found in a field outside York with no identification, no wallet, but we found a library card which led us to your address.'

'Yes,' Nigel Post sighed, 'James used my address as an accommodation address. It had a permanency about it, whereas he could never settle in one address, in the early days he moved from rented flat to rented flat as if he was looking for something and hoped to find it in the next flat he moved into. So it was easier to use my address for things like library membership . . . and he just kept up the practice.'

'I see.'

'I didn't mind. It enabled me to keep track of him. He was my brother . . . a complete wastrel, but my brother just the same.'

'Was he employed?'

'No, he virtually never worked all his life, never had a job.'

'Never?'

'Couldn't hold down any proper half decent job . . . tried his hand at self-employment but that was a disaster. Any jobs he did have was cash in hand labouring sort of work. He never seemed to accept adulthood, always dressing in the clothes he wore as a young man.'

'We noticed his shoes.'

'That's exactly what I mean. We both suffered from a lack

of height. I am just five foot tall . . . both left school early but I got a job and held it down, Department of Highways, local authority, very safe, pays nothing but me and my wife could afford the rent on our house. We didn't have children.'

'I see.'

'But James, he just came and went, never knew what he did . . . then the drink took him.'

'Oh?'

'Yes, he was in a bad way with the drink for about ten years. That was a bad time. He became down-and-out, begging for money, filthy clothes. I shudder to think what went down his throat in those years . . . poison soup, but that is often the way of it.'

'Yes.'

'In this case, he was set upon, beaten up by a gang of youths; small, smelly guy, easy target. He got one hell of a kicking but he was hospitalized, cleaned up, fed properly while the broken bones healed and he dried out. Sober for the first time in years. The hospital contacted me when he was due to be discharged . . . I never knew he had been admitted. He only gave them my address when he was about to be discharged. They had incinerated all his clothing as representing a health hazard, he needed some replacement kit so I looked out some of my old clothes and brought them to the hospital, and then dragged him to an AA meeting and sat with him throughout. To his credit he went back, and kept going back and kept dry. He even had a long term girlfriend . . . and took a council tenancy, and they had a son, but they split up after a while. Still never held down a job but he kept dry. So that was a big thing.'

'Good for him.'

'Yes, for him that was an achievement as I said, one man's floor being another man's ceiling. For him to stay dry was a big deal, a very big deal.'

'Yes, I can understand that. Do you know of anyone who would want to harm him?'

'I'm afraid I don't. I knew little of his life. I suspect it was not very ... well ... small guy, no employment to speak of. I suspect it was a quiet life he led. I knew of no friends and I knew of no enemies.'

'I see.' Hennessey tapped his notepad with his ballpoint. 'Do you know what Mr Post's last known address was?'

'I have a note of it at home ... but yes ... I have a note of it.'

Carmen Pharoah and Thomson Ventnor walked up the inclined drive to the Malpass home in Hutton Cranswick. The house itself was interwar, large, two storeys, red-tiled roof, generous garden, noted Ventnor, very generous, as he pressed the doorbell. The bell rang a conventional double tone and did so loudly, so loudly that Ventnor did not think it appropriate to press the bell a second time. The door was opened, confidently so, soon upon the bell sounding, by an elegant seeming woman in her mid fifties, Pharoah estimated, who was dressed fetchingly in a yellow knee-length dress and white court shoes. She smiled warmly at the officers, 'Mr and Mrs Blackhouse? You are a trifle early, but no matter, do come in.' She stepped to one side. Pharoah and Ventnor remained stationary and stone-faced as they showed the woman their identity cards. 'Police,' Ventnor said flatly.

'Oh.' The woman's face fell; her hand went up to her mouth. 'I hope there's no trouble.'

'Plenty,' Ventnor replaced his identity card in his wallet. 'There's always plenty of trouble but probably not for this house.'

'How can I help?'

'We'd like to speak to Mr Malpass, if he is at home.'

'Yes ... yes he is. I am Mrs Malpass by the way. Do come in. We are waiting for a Mr and Mrs Blackhouse, they have been referred to us.'

'Referred to you?' Carmen Pharoah stepped across the threshold of the house.

'Yes, we offer an alcohol abuse counselling service.'

'I see.'

'But . . . well . . . come in. My husband is in the living room, second door on the left.'

Carmen Pharoah, followed by Thomson Ventnor walked into the living room. A tall, well-dressed man stood as they entered. Carmen Pharoah read the room; she saw it neat, tastefully furnished with dark but highly patterned carpet, furniture covered in pastel shades of blues, with blue tinted wallpaper. The bay window looked out on to an equally neatly kept garden, surrounded on all sides by a ten foot high privet.

'The police, dear,' Mrs Malpass announced.

The man stepped forward and extended his hand. 'Ronald Malpass. This is my wife, Sylvia. How can we help?' He was smartly dressed in white trousers, summer shoes, blue tee shirt.

'Just a little information, please,' Ventnor replied, noting how tall Malpass was, over six feet he guessed.

'In that case, please take a seat do.' He indicated the chairs and settee in the room as he resumed his seat in the armchair he had been occupying when the officers had entered. Pharoah and Ventnor sat side by side on the settee and Mrs Malpass sat in the vacant armchair. Carmen Pharoah thought Ronald Malpass overly confident and she also noticed a certain look of worry across Mrs Malpass's eyes.

'We understand you know, or knew, a lady called Angela Prebble?'

'Angie . . . Angela . . .' Ronald Malpass sat back in the armchair. 'That's a name I have not heard for a while. She disappeared, I believe . . . some years ago.'

'Yes, she did,' Ventnor replied. 'She's reappeared.'

'Oh . . .' Malpass looked alert, interested. 'How is she?'

'Deceased.'

Sylvia Malpass gasped. Ronald Malpass's brow knitted.

He remained silent for a few moments and then asked, 'What happened?'

'We don't know but she has been identified as being one of the bodies found at Bromyards.'

'Bromyards?' Malpass queried.

'The big house,' Sylvia Malpass explained. 'It's been on the news . . . in the papers.'

'Ah . . . yes, of course. Oh dear, poor Angela . . . we did wonder.'

'How did you know her?'

'Socially . . . not really very close but we knew her.'

'How? How did you know her?'

'Socially. As I said.'

'Can you be a bit more specific, please?'

'We were in the same bunch of people, the same group.'

Carmen Pharoah sighed, 'If you could be . . .'

'Alcoholics Anonymous,' Sylvia Malpass explained. Then she addressed her husband. 'It was going to come out.'

'Thank you,' Carmen Pharoah smiled at Sylvia Malpass. 'No shame there, alcoholism is a disease . . . no shame at all.'

'There shouldn't be,' Ronald Malpass added, 'but there is the stigma, it's always there. But I am dry now . . . we both are.' He held his right hand outstretched, palm down, fingers pressed together. 'Rock steady,' he said with a note of pride in his voice. 'I couldn't have done that at one time, I would have been shaking like a leaf. Dried out about fifteen years ago, before that there is a ten year gap in my memory, can't remember a thing I did in those ten years . . . but now . . . I still enjoy the sensation of waking up with a clear head.'

'Good for you,' Thomson Ventnor said. 'I know it can be quite a battle.'

'Yes. Why? Are you . . .'

'No,' Ventnor said. 'I'm not.'

'So,' Carmen Pharoah attempted to pull the conversation back to the relevancy of their visit. 'Angela Prebble was in Alcoholics Anonymous?'

'Yes, she was.'

'And that was the extent of you knowing her?'

'More or less . . . well . . . we became friends but not close friends. She was from the West Coast of Scotland and had difficulty settling in Yorkshire, though I confess you do hear Scottish accents quite a lot in Yorkshire, in the pubs and the shops.'

'You go into pubs?'

'Oh yes,' Malpass smiled. 'Why not? I enjoy pubs . . . I . . . we . . . Sylvia and I, just don't touch alcohol but pubs are enjoyable places. We are aware that just one drop of alcohol and we'd both be off the wagon. We watch each other.'

'So we met Angela at AA and then met socially outside AA meetings, a coffee and a chat, but that's all.'

'Very well.'

'Now we do our own thing. We offer alcohol abuse counselling, on a one-to-one, or couple-to-couple basis. Have you ever been to an AA meeting?'

'Can't say I have,' Ventnor said.

'Me neither.' Carmen Pharoah noticed a pleasant scent of furniture polish in the room, not too strong, not over-powering, but there, in the background.

'Well, they are large . . . as the name implies, very anonymous and that suits many folk, but we found that others need to feel more like individuals with personalities and identities, and need one-to-one or couple-to-couple support and advice. So we thought we'd offer our experience to others. We let AA know and they refer people to us . . . in fact we are . . .'

'Yes, Mr Malpass,' Pharoah interrupted him. 'We'll be on our way soon. Did you see Angela Prebble at all around the time of her disappearance?'

'I can't recall. It was a long time ago you see . . . years . . . ten years. I really don't know how long ago it was . . . I think I was sober then.'

'You were,' Sylvia Malpass smiled warmly. 'You had to have been, we met her in an AA meeting, you'd stopped drinking.'

'Of course, I had gotten sober; I was a dry alky by then. We joined a drink watchers group which was a spin off from mainstream AA.'

'Drink watchers?'

'Yes, we didn't need the AA approach, "Hello, I'm Ronald and I'm an alcoholic"; we just needed human company to help fill up the evenings, but not necessarily talk about our battle with the bottle. So we'd meet in cafes. In the summer we'd go for walks along the river. We just helped each other get through those awful hours from five until eight p.m. We found that if we could reach eight p.m. without a drink then the desire went. It wasn't for everyone, some folk drank at home at any time of the day or night, but if you drank because you needed human company and then the drink took you, then our little group was a good place to be . . . human contact, a chat, but we kept each other off the booze.'

'Very good.'

'So we'd get through until eight and then disperse and meet up again a couple of evenings later.'

'Not every evening?'

'No, we couldn't sustain that. If one of our group could not get through the evening they could go to an AA meeting.'

'Quite a lifeless house, I thought.' Carmen Pharoah drove slowly away from the Malpass house.

'Sort of,' Ventnor glanced to his left at a 1930s' Rolls Royce parked sedately in the driveway of a neighbouring house. 'Dead . . . lifeless as you say. No plants . . . no books on the shelves.'

'And alcohol is an issue again. This entire investigation is looking like it's booze related.'

It was Saturday, 15.37 hours.

FIVE

Sunday, 14th June – 09.15 hours – 21.45 hours
*in which two inquiries converge and the kind reader
hears of Thomson Ventnor's private issues.*

Hennessey reclined in his chair. 'Booze, the demon drink,' he sighed and raised his eyebrows.

'Seems a likely thread, sir, a likely common denominator,' Carmen Pharoah sipped her tea. 'Veronica Goodwin evidently had a significant problem, so did Angela Prebble and Mr Penta was angry about being abandoned in favour of AA . . . and alcohol may also explain the unidentified victim, a woman in her sixties, I think she was.'

'Yes, sixty-one plus or minus twelve months,' Hennessey glanced at the ever expanding file, 'just the sort of elderly down-and-out, an old soak who would not be missed, who had probably wandered into a different part of the country to avoid the shame of being as she was where she was known; came to York to be an unknown in a strange town so we have no record of her on our mis per files.' He tapped the desk top. 'I've said it before and I'll say it again, the sooner we get a National Missing Person's Database the better, and I can't see why it should not be set up in these high-tech information technology days, seems to be the easiest thing in the world if you ask me. Well, enough of my ramblings for this fine, sunny Sunday morning. So it seems that we might have a breakthrough. We still have yet to notify all the next of kin and obtain confirmation of ID of all the victims. As I understand it, the families of Paula Rees, Rosemary Arkwright, Helena Tunicliffe, Roslyn Farmfield and Denise Clay have yet to be visited. We can address that now. I don't like making first contact in situations like this by phone, very insensitive, but it may be expedient.'

'A simple phone call asking if their missing family member had a significant drink problem. We can follow up with a home visit later to explain the reason for our interest and obtain help to confirm identification,' Carmen Pharoah suggested eagerly, 'and also ask if they had any contact with the York Chapter of AA.'

'Good. Can you get on that?'

'Yes, sir.'

'So what have you got on, Yellich?'

'Working with the Crown Prosecution Service to frame the charges for the Askham Links manslaughter case but, unlike us, they don't work on Sundays, so I am at your disposal for any legwork.'

'Good. Ventnor?'

'Theft of prestige cars, sir.'

'Oh, yes . . . any progress?'

'Little to report, sir, but they're getting bolder, they'll make a mistake.'

'Yes, so you have time as of now for this case.' Hennessey tapped the file of the Bromyards murders.

'Yes, sir.'

'Good. Webster?'

'I also have time, sir. I am working on the burglaries of wealthy homes in the area, same MO and, like Ventnor, I am waiting for them to make a mistake.'

'All right . . . you see . . .' Hennessey leaned forward and clasped his hands together, resting them on his desktop, 'I don't know how best to prioritize this, you see we have a code forty-one on our hands.'

'A murder!' Yellich sat forward in his chair. 'As if the Bromyards case wasn't enough.'

'Yes. You were all committed yesterday and so I attended the murder scene. He . . . the victim, was an old,

well oldish . . . a man in his middle years . . . positively
identified as one James Post . . . strangled, head smashed
in, found in a field just outside the city. Probably would
be lying there still had not an alert member of the public
put two and two together when she saw a column of flies
hovering over something. I'll explain what I mean later,
but the upshot of it is we have to visit his drum, an address
on the Tang Hall Estate, so not a wealthy man. His brother,
who identified the body, phoned later with his brother's
address. He also has a key but I asked him to stay clear,
it's going to be a lowlife petty criminal murder, brought
on by some petty quarrel. It's nothing of the magnitude
of this,' Hennessey patted the Bromyards murders file again,
'but it's fresh, we're still within the first twenty-four hours,
whereas with the Bromyards case we seem to be coming in
when it's all over, no fresh evidence at all.' Hennessey fell
silent. 'I am going to the post-mortem of James Post; Dr
D'Acre is coming in today to do it, to the delight of her
daughters.' He smiled. 'She told me that if she is at work
on the weekends her daughters get to ride their horse, without
having to compete with her . . . more time for them you see.
But I have a visit to do before then . . . that name . . . the
couple you visited yesterday afternoon, Pharoah and
Ventnor . . . Malpass?'

'Yes.'

'That name rang bells with me and yesterday evening
when I was exercising my dog I remembered. So, visit,
then the post-mortem for me. Webster.'

'Sir.'

'I want you to go with Ventnor, collect the key from
James Post's brother and visit his flat.'

'Yes, sir.'

'DC Phaorah, if you could address the phone calls you
suggested?'

'Yes, sir.'

*   *   *

The woman's face melted into a smile when she saw that it was George Hennessey who had knocked on her door. 'George,' she said warmly and bent forward to kiss his cheek.

'How are you, Tilly?'

'Getting there . . . do come in.'

'Thanks.' Hennessey swept off his panama and stepped over the threshold into Matilda Pakenham's house in Holgate. He saw that she kept it in a neat and clean manner and was burning a joss stick, which filled the house with the pleasant scent of incense.

'Are you studying?' Hennessey noted a pile of text books in the corner of the living room as he accepted her invitation to take a seat.

'Yes,' she smiled proudly, 'just as I said I would if I got the chance . . . History, no firm plans as to what to do with the degree once I get it, but early days yet. I feel like an old woman when I attend lectures with all those female students who were in school uniform just a year ago.'

'You are younger than you are old, Tilly,' Hennessey smiled. 'If you see what I mean.'

'Thanks.'

'Any news of the ex?'

'No, he seems to be leaving me alone. He didn't enjoy gaol, he couldn't charm the guys in there.'

'Well, not only am I calling on you to see how you have settled . . .'

'Settled is the word. If you hadn't bought me that meal that day I'd still be wrapped in a blanket in a shop doorway, picking out Edelweiss on that old tin whistle for a few coins in a plastic beaker.' She shuddered. 'What a place to fall to . . . but they say that . . . they say you have to reach your gutter before you can start the long climb back to respectable living.'

'That's what Alcoholics Anonymous say.'

'Yes, good people . . . they helped me as much as you did.'

'It's actually that which I have called to ask you about.'

'Oh?'

'Yes, I want to pick your brains.'

'I'll make us some tea.' She rose from the scatter cushion on which she sat. 'My brain will make for richer pickings if I am drinking tea. Join me, George?'

'Love to, thank you.'

Once again settled, each with a mug of herbal tea, which was not to George Hennessey's taste, he said, 'I recall you talking about a couple . . . one Mr and Mrs Malpass.'

Tilly Pakenham shuddered. 'Yes, I will never forget them . . . oh . . . will I ever.'

'Tell me about them.'

'Why? Have they come to your attention? I knew they would.'

'Just tell me about them . . . how you met . . . why you didn't see them again? If you recall, you told me once. I was not really interested in them then.'

'But you are now?'

'Well, let's just say, let's just say things have developed.'

'I see . . . well Ronald and Sylvia, what can I tell you? We met in an AA meeting. They were different from the others, they had confidence, self-respect. If they were alcoholics they had made a full recovery. Not just dry, but they had recovered their self-confidence, self-respect, self-worth. He was tall and handsome and she was elegant . . . both well dressed. In fact, he put me in mind of my husband, the charming salesman and equally vicious wife beater. He wouldn't have sold as many cars and kitchen units as he did if the customers knew how often he put my blood on the wall.'

'Indeed.' Hennessey sipped the herbal tea.

'Well, they approached me and said they offered an alternative for one or two evenings a week, and I asked them what they meant. They said that it's more of a drink avoidance group . . . for people who get fed up with the usual

AA routine of people boasting how they overcame it. It does get routine and they said it came to the point that they realized that they were sitting in the AA meetings as a means of avoiding sitting in a pub. It was seen as an alternative place to go, but you had to sit in rows like you were in a cinema and listen to one or two people's life stories, and what they really needed was a pleasant evening's chat, like spending the evening in the pub with your mates but without the alcohol.'

'All right.'

'Well, it sounded inviting, so I went along, met in a cafe in the centre of York, one that opens in the evening, and we drank coffee, had a nibble to eat and just chatted until we felt we had killed the evening, by which time we just wanted to go home and sleep.'

'Just the three of you?'

'Oh no . . . no . . . there could have been six or seven sometimes, but those two were always there, it was their group, Ronald and Sylvia's . . . and a small bloke who rarely said much. I can't remember his name, but Ron and Sylvia were all charm and smiles and approving looks, and it's that which got me on edge. I had just escaped from a man who had lured me into a violent marriage with exactly that selfsame sort of charm and approval.'

A heavy footfall was heard passing the window, a click, click, click of steel-heeled stilettos which echoed in the narrow street. 'That woman,' Tilly Pakenham inclined her head to the window, 'she lives three doors down. I tell you, she can't go into her backyard to put her rubbish out or hang her washing on the line without wearing those shoes, so that the whole terrace hears her. When she walks out of doors the world has to know about it.'

'It could be worse,' Hennessey drained his cup, 'could be a lot worse.'

'Dare say. So, where was I?'

'The charming Ronald.'

'Ah, yes . . . and the equally charming Sylvia, they were like two peas in a pod.'

'How long did you attend their evening get-togethers?'

'For a few months over one winter.'

'And you stopped going?'

'Yes, when they asked me if I'd like to go to the coast with them . . . just a day's run to the coast.'

'In winter?'

'Yes. I thought that was strange. I saw a small palm tree in a hailstorm once . . . winter hail . . . that is a coastal resort in the winter, so I didn't think it sounded inviting, and then there was that smile . . . that charm . . . alarm bells rang. I thought, I've been here before, so I declined, and when I did a look of anger flashed across his eyes and I knew then that I had made the right choice.'

'Did he extend the invitation to others?'

'Not on that occasion, that evening there was only myself, the quiet little guy and Ronald and Sylvia. It was when the little guy had gone to buy more coffee for us that they asked me if I wanted to go with them to the coast for the day. That was the last I saw of them.'

'I see. When was that?'

'Oh . . . about two winters ago.'

'Do you remember anyone else there?'

'One or two, mostly women, varying ages.'

'Any in particular?'

'Yes, a really sweet girl called Veronica, she came quite often then just stopped, probably got the same sort of vibes off Ronald and Sylvia that I got.'

'Yes,' Hennessey rose from his chair. 'She probably did.'

Dr D'Acre pushed the microphone away from her and up towards the ceiling, it being mounted on a long anglepoise arm, and peeled off her latex gloves as Eric Filey wheeled the corpse of the late James Post towards the mortuary. 'Well, that's it,' she announced calmly, 'massive head

injuries and also massive injuries to the throat. Someone
wanted him deceased all right, and frankly either injury
would have been fatal.'

'A belt and bracer job,' Hennessey offered. He stood
against the wall of the mortuary laboratory dressed in green
disposable paper coveralls.

'Yes . . . yes . . . I dare say that you could say that, dare
say you could describe it thusly . . . a belt and bracers job.
The injuries are certainly contemporary with each other and
I would guess, but only guess, that he was strangled before
sustaining the head injury, though . . . though . . . there is no
reason why they have to be in that order, but it was someone
making sure . . . belt and bracers job as you say. Total
absence of blood under his fingernails. He didn't put up
much of a fight, or he clawed at nothing, or couldn't fight
at all, so perhaps the blow to the head was the first injury
to be sustained after all . . . but a blow to the head has more
of a making sure feel about it than does strangulation.'

'Yes, I would think the same.'

'If he was strangled by someone much larger than he,
then that would also help explain the absence of blood; he
simply could not reach his attacker's face and being a very
small man that means that his attacker would not have to
be abnormally tall . . . he might have tried to pull his
attacker's hands off him but he wouldn't have clawed at
them . . . people in that situation just don't.'

'I see.'

'His kidneys have been damaged by alcohol consump-
tion over many years and his liver showed signs of recovery
from alcohol damage. Very useful organ is the liver, in that
it can recover from sustained abuse . . . the kidneys can't.
So he was a dried out alcoholic. His body was clean, he
washed, but the kidney damage was unmissable, he had hit
the bottle in his life and the bottle had hit back.'

'Very well.'

'So tell me,' Dr D'Acre turned to Hennessey, 'have you

identified the last remaining unidentified corpse in the kitchen garden murders case?'

'No. Not yet.'

'I see . . . that will be another grave for me to visit.'

'Another?'

'Yes, I visit John Brown's grave from time to time . . . you recall the bloated floater?'

'Ah, yes . . . you evacuated this room, put on all extractor fans, took a deep breath, stabbed the stomach and ran for the door?'

'Yes, that one. He was given a name and buried in a pauper's grave in Fulford Cemetery, but he was somebody's son, possibly somebody's brother, maybe somebody's father . . . so they gave him a name and buried him, and I go and lay a flower on his grave every now and again. So I might be doing the same for that wretched woman. Just sufficient of her remained for me to be able to tell that her liver and kidneys were shot to hell; just a derelict bag lady, no one missed her. But she was somebody's daughter, maybe somebody's sister, and possibly somebody's mother and no one reported her missing. She'll be given a name and buried in the paupers section of the cemetery close to John Brown . . . another grave for me to visit.'

Webster turned the key in the lock of James Post's flat. Ventnor stood beside him. Both officers wore latex gloves. Without a word passing between them the two officers entered the flat, which was on the second floor of a block of low rise flats and accessed from a neatly kept common staircase. They proceeded with caution and with Webster announcing their presence by calling out 'Police'. Receiving no answer, the officers stepped into the corridor carefully observing the six foot rule, that they must continually be within six feet of each other at all times to witness any findings of evidence, and to witness that neither was light-fingered should the householder or relative accuse the police of theft.

The flat had five rooms and a bathroom and a kitchen, three of the rooms being bedrooms. It was clearly not a flat intended for single person occupancy. The possibility which occurred to both Webster and Ventnor was that James Post was once married, his spouse and children had left and he had retained the tenancy, as would have been his right, and he would have resisted all moves by the Housing Department to accept a smaller flat, tenants rights being tenants rights.

The sitting room of the flat was found to be airless, with all windows closed, and in an untidy and unclean state. As so often, during the summer months, the fireplace had become a receptacle for all things inflammable, awaiting the first chill of autumn before being ignited. The furniture was inexpensive, covered with a fine layer of dust and the carpet was sticky to walk on. Two of the bedrooms had beds without bedding and wardrobes which proved, upon inspection, to be empty. The third, and largest, bedroom contained a double bed covered with crumpled sheets and there was male clothing strewn liberally about the floor and atop a chest of drawers.

'Definitely a teenager,' growled Webster.

'Sorry?'

'Well, the Chief's recording stated he wore youthful clothing and footwear, and clearly still hasn't learned to tidy his room.'

Ventnor laughed softly. 'Reminds me of a sticker I once saw on a teenager's bedroom door, "Why should I tidy my room when your generation has made such a mess of the world?"'

'Hard to argue with that.' Webster turned and stepped from the room and Ventnor followed, to complete the 'sweep' before commencing a detailed drawer by drawer, shelf by shelf, cupboard by cupboard, search of James Post's home. The officers opened the door of the last of the rooms to be entered and stopped short at the threshold. The room was a small box room or store room close to the entrance of the flat. It had no natural light and smelled strongly of chemicals. Webster switched on the light which glowed a soft red. A bench ran across one wall containing phials of chemicals, film negatives hung by clothes pegs from a length of cord which was suspended from wall to wall across the room.

'Well, now we know how he spent his free time,' Webster commented.

'Serious kit,' Ventnor said.

'The plastic tools?'

'No . . . that,' Ventnor pointed to a camera lying on the bench furthest from the well, 'a Nikon I think, very nice piece of kit.'

'You're a photographer?'

'Hardly, just dabble in it, but I know enough to know I'd be hard pressed to afford a camera like that.'

'I see.'

'But it's at odds with the rest of the contents of the flat, everything is cheap and tacky.'

'Stolen, you think?'

'Possibly, or he might have bought it, if he had a little undeclared business going on here . . . printing naughty pics, the sort that folk wouldn't want to send to the chemists . . .'

'Where would he keep any prints?'

'Somewhere flat, like the inside of a drawer or an album . . . even a large envelope, somewhere out of natural light which will make prints fade.'

A drawer underneath the bench on which the developing chemicals stood did indeed contain a number of large padded envelopes, which contained prints of a risqué nature, as Ventnor suggested, not the sort of film one would send to the high street chemist to develop, but one envelope caught his eye, it was labelled 'Bromyards'. He picked it up gingerly and pointed the label out to Ventnor, 'Small world,' he said.

'Wheels within wheels,' Ventnor gasped.

Webster took the photographs from the envelope. Each photograph was of one of the victims of the Bromyards kitchen garden murders, all were naked, all were attached by their ankle to the length of chain. Some of the victims had a blank expression as if accepting their fate, others displayed a look of extreme fear, others were pleading with their eyes . . . and each was labelled by name on the reverse of the print, each with their full name: Angela Prebble . . . Veronica Goodwin . . . save for one which seemed to the officers to be a photograph of the one victim that had not been identified, who was known to Post as simply 'Old Annie'. 'Old Annie' had clearly kept her identity a closely guarded secret, even to the end.

The two officers laid the photographs on the bench and withdrew from the room, and from the flat, touching as little as they could.

Webster went calmly but quickly down the stairs and out into the gardens at the front of the building to contact DCI Hennessey on his mobile phone, to notify him of the discovery in James Post's flat and request his attendance and the attendance of scene of crime officers. Ventnor began to knock on the doors of the neighbours of James Post, and found he took an instant dislike to the first woman who opened her door upon his calling. It was her eyes, he thought, all in her eyes. The woman seemed to be smirking at him. So natural was her look that Ventnor guessed she would probably be smirking at the world, as if it was all a joke and all beneath her in some way, as though she was above all, superior to all; her and her little flat on the Tang Hall Estate of the city of York where the tourists never venture.

'Don't know much about him,' she said, smiling with her eyes and her mouth as if she was giving an eager to please act, thought Ventnor, but he also sensed that she was about to burst into laughter at his expense, and she also seemed to know that she was annoying him and delighted in doing so. She was, he sensed, the sort of woman who would provoke any male partner to punch her. 'He was just the little man across the landing who didn't say much and who kept strange hours . . . strange man with strange hours.'

'Oh?'

'Yes, coming and going at all hours of the day and night. He used to have a drink problem many years ago, that's why she left him.'

'She?'

'A woman and her children. They were not married, they cohabited.'

'Did you see anyone call . . . any friends, for example?'

'Him! With friends?' She snorted with laughter. 'He just kept himself to himself, never even knocked on my door to borrow a drop of milk if he ran out of the stuff. He was the quiet man on the stair but always seemed preoccupied.'

'But you don't know with what?'

'No, not in the twenty years I have been here. The others on the stair will probably say the same about him. Ask them if you like.'

'Don't worry,' Ventnor turned away, 'we will.' Then he turned back and asked of the woman as an afterthought, 'Did Mr Post own a car?'

'No.' The woman answered clearly. 'He walked from his home and walked back. I never even saw him get out of a car, or into one as a passenger.'

Somerled Yellich handed the photographs back to Hennessey, all printed in black and white on coarse matt finish, sixteen prints, some of which showed a victim, clearly a victim, a middle-aged man or woman, dressed in ill-fitting rags, the men with distinct facial hair and all with matted scalp hair, all lying or kneeling or on all fours, all with that look of resignation or despair or bewilderment, which was also in the eyes of the victims photographed in the kitchen garden at

Bromyards. Yet, in the photographs of the victims taken out of doors, the photographer had clearly knelt to get the camera angle level with the eyes, so that he not only captured the look therein but also a distinct landmark. In one, the background showed the unmistakable outline of the Forth Railway Bridge, another showed the entrance to the Box Railway Tunnel in Wiltshire. Yet another showing Boston Stump in Lincolnshire, and yet another which showed not a famous landmark but a road signpost which was easily distinguished and read 'St Mabyn – 1 mile'.

'St Mabyn?' Hennessey queried taking back the prints from Yellich.

'It's in Cornwall, boss. I looked it up in my road atlas.'

'Cornwall,' Hennessey sighed, 'Cornwall . . . so we have Scotland, Wiltshire, Lincolnshire and Cornwall, as well as others whose landmarks have still to be identified.'

'Yes, sir . . . and then five showing no body at all, just Post standing in a Hindley-esque manner, looking down at the ground on which he is standing, and, like Myra Hindley, he seems to have favoured moorland.'

'Yes, sir, and also like Hindley, he is unlikely to have taken those pictures of himself by himself. It's possible with a delayed shutter mechanism, but the remoteness of all the locations and Post did not drive . . . he had an accomplice or accomplices.'

'Yes.' Hennessey looked at the five photographs which just showed James Post, small, diminutive, standing over a small plot of land which clearly had some dreadful significance for him, but a significance, despite its dread nature, which was evidently also a source of pride for him.

'So we have twenty-five victims and that is the twenty-five which they catalogued. There'll be more.'

'Yes, sir.'

'We need to know more about James Post.'

'Yes, sir.'

'He's the key to this.'

'Yes, sir.' Yellich stood.

'I am going to take learned advice.'

'Understood, sir.'

'If . . . if . . . your enquiries about James Post lead to the mention of a name Malpass, let me know immediately.'

'Malpass, sir?'

'Yes, Mr and Mrs Malpass. If you do hear mention of that name I want to know and I'll tell you why at that point.'

'We have interviewed them, sir. Ventnor and Pharoah . . .'

'I know,' Hennessey smiled. 'I know.'

'But if they're suspects we should move before they kill again . . . surely?' Yellich's voice rose.

'No . . .' Hennessey leaned back in his chair. 'They are not suspects, not yet, and if I am right there's no more danger.'

'No danger, sir? They're serial killers!'

'Yes . . . and their last victim was James Post. If I am right, it's all been happening around us without us knowing anything about it and we have come in at the aftermath. But I want to bounce my thoughts off a learned brain before I decide how to proceed. And I need more on James Post. Get Webster on it with you.'

Webster thought Mrs Lismore to be a kindly lady. She seemed warm of manner, she was a woman whose eyes sparkled and her smile seemed to Webster to be genuine. She was slender and short, with close cropped hair, and stood on the threshold of her house on the Tang Hall Estate having fully opened the door. 'I was,' she said, 'until I moved out . . . I am Mrs Lismore now. This is going back some years. How did you find me?'

'Housing Department,' Webster said, 'when I told them it was an important investigation.'

'All right, well now you've found me. Would you like to come in? Better than standing out here, even on a pleasant day like today.'

The inside of Mrs Lismore's flat was, Webster found, neat and clean, though a little Spartan and spoke of a limited income. Webster accepted her invitation to sit down. 'I told them my partner was abusive,' Mrs Lismore explained as she too settled into an armchair, 'and I let them assume I meant physically abusive, and so they rehoused me and the children here . . . just a few streets away but he never bothers us.'

'He won't be bothering you ever again anyway.'

'Oh . . .?' Colour drained from her face. 'You're not telling me he's dead?'

'Yes, I am. He was found deceased in a field outside York. We traced him by a library card in his pocket and his brother made the identification.'

'Oh . . .'

'But we need to know as much about him as possible. We believe he might have been involved in a serious crime which we are still investigating.'

'I see . . . that's unlike him, he was an alcoholic and that's why I left, just picked up the children I had had with my husband and walked into the Housing Department and said, "I have walked out of an abusive relationship". They put us in a woman's shelter and then allocated me this tenancy. So, he was a drinker but never a criminal. I do find that surprising.'

'It probably was a development in his life which occurred after you left him,' Webster suggested, 'but the manner of Mr Post's death suggests he was a deliberate target, he was not a random victim who was in the wrong place at the wrong time.'

'What was the manner . . . can I ask?'

'Strangled and then battered to death, and his identification removed from his person.'

'But they missed the library card?'

'Yes.'

'I see . . . certainly sounds like someone wanted him dead, I'll give you that.'

'So, accepting you had little or nothing to do with Mr Post in the last few years . . . but might you know of any enemies he had?'

'No . . . no I don't'

'Friends?'

'Again, no. I do wish I could help. He drove any friends he might have had away from him.'

'How did he deal with his drink problem?'

'Alcoholics Anonymous . . . eventually. It was a long time before he got round to going there, but in the end he went and they helped him stay off the bottle . . . so I heard.'

'Long shot, but we had to ask.'

'My son could help you . . . well, he might be able to.'

'Your son?'

'Kenneth. He works in the Civil Service. Nothing special, fairly low grade and money's tight for him . . . State Pensions Department on the Stonebow. He is Jim Post's natural son but he took my name. I believe he tried to get to know his father in the last year or so once he . . . his father . . . had dried out.'

Kamella 'Kamy' Joseph was a slender woman of striking Asian features, with long black hair. She sat in her office at the university with a large poster of Sydney Opera House stuck to the wall behind her. She glanced out of the window at ducks on the pond and then turned to Hennessey and said, 'I think you are quite correct. It's all over.'

'It seemed like the normal progression, easy victims and undervalued people who won't be missed . . .'

'Yes, the photographs are clearly of down-and-outs and seem to be deposited or buried all over the UK. I mean, why should the Lothian Borders Police link this gentleman here with this gentleman found in Lincolnshire? Presume they had no identification on them?'

'It's safe to assume they didn't, otherwise the other police forces would have contacted us, and they do not appear to have done, but we think this murder spree is about twenty years in existence . . . or was if they have stopped.'

'If the man in these photographs has himself been murdered in the same way these other victims were murdered then yes, they have stopped. This is going to make an interesting paper. I would appreciate having a look at the evidence once it is all wrapped up.'

'I think that could be arranged.'

'Thank you . . . and then they ratcheted things up by abducting people who would be missed and leaving them together in an overgrown kitchen garden.'

'Taunting us?'

'Possibly, possibly even a way of giving themselves up. I have a photograph of a crime scene in the United States of a serial killer's work . . . or activity. This man would get into the houses or apartments of women who lived alone, murder them, and then ransack the property. In the home of one of his victims he got her lipstick and on the mirror of her dressing table he wrote, "Stop me before I do this again".'

'Blimey.'

'Yes, he wanted to be stopped but he couldn't just walk into a police station . . . the strange workings of the human mind, but that incident has lead to the theory that when a serial killer, or killers, appear to be getting bolder and taking valued and well integrated people as their victims, it is a way of giving themselves up . . . of stopping it all.'

'Interesting . . . because they want the notoriety?'

'Who knows why? It is the thrust of forensic psychology to try to get into the minds of these people, to identify some pathology which they have in common. Being unable, yet wanting to stop has been claimed by other serial killers, so it might not be about notoriety at all.'

'What sort of person or persons are we looking for?'

Kamella Joseph PhD by the nameplate on her desk, reclined in her chair. 'Well, apart from the usual manipulation by charm, which is common among psychopaths, I'd say you're looking for someone . . . or persons . . . who could offer these victims what they seemed to want, which would appear to be acceptance. Down-and-outs are continually shunned, yet if a charming person, who is well dressed and is like the down-and-out wants to be like, offers friendship, and if that hand of alleged friendship is taken . . .'

'The trap closes.'

'Yes,' Kamella Joseph smiled, 'the trap closes.'

'And if someone is not a down-and-out but feels socially isolated . . .?'

'Same thing, the offer to meet unmet needs.'

'Lucky Matilda Pakenham.'

'Who's she?'

'A young woman who, when at a low point of her life, declined the offer of a trip to the coast with a charming couple who had befriended her.'

'Ah . . . so you have a suspect or a couple of suspects?'

'Yes, but so far just suspects, and I don't want to act too soon . . . don't want to put them to flight . . . though I think there is little risk of that, but I don't want to run the risk . . . and I think . . . I believe . . . that they have taken their last victim anyway.'

'Only ever saw him with another woman once . . . just one time.' The man sat rigidly in his chair of grey painted steel, with shallow grey upholstery, behind a metal desk of two-tone grey. 'He didn't notice me. I wasn't looking for him; we just passed in the street, father and son, we just walked past each other, but he'd cleaned himself up. No longer an alcoholic, he was smart and clean and tidy.' Kenneth Lismore was his father's son, Webster thought, very small, slightly built, but he had benefited from his mother's influence, because here was the same benevolent attitude, the same warmth about the eyes.

'Go on,' Webster prodded gently.

'Well, we met up after that. I wanted to get to know him,

now that he had sobered, and so we met for coffee from time to time. I asked him about the woman I had seen him with on Swinegate and he said it was a friend of his. He didn't want me to meet her, he said that "we understood each other", and added "but it's not serious". I took that to mean that they had both been alcoholics, and she did indeed appear to have a hardbitten and a used look about her.'

'A lady of the streets, perhaps?'

'Possibly, but by then helping each other to lead cleaner, more sober lives . . . so good for both of them, but she still had a humourless expression and cold, angry eyes. All that I saw in an instant.'

'A name?'

'He did mention her name once, but you'll know her.'

'Oh?'

'Most probably, she had gaol house tatts.'

'Gaol house tatts?'

'Just here,' Lismore tapped the top of his left hand. 'Girls in residential care often give themselves similar sorts of tattoos. Soak a ball of cotton wool in ink and push a pin through it, then prick, prick, prick or rather jab, jab, jab and the pin takes the ink beneath the surface of the skin and there it remains.'

'Ah, yes, of course, I know the type. Will you look at some photographs?'

'Yes, of course, but this was a few years ago, blonde hair stiff with peroxide . . . she had a name . . . what did dad call her?' Lismore turned his head to one side and glanced out at the concrete and glass that was the Stonebow development in the centre of York. 'What was her name? It was a racecourse name . . .'

'She had the name of a racecourse?'

'No . . . no . . .' Kenneth Lismore held up his hand, 'part of a racecourse followed her name, like "Winning Post Mary", but not that name . . . a name like it "Starting Gate Sally" . . . something like that.'

'First bend?' Webster suggested.

Kenneth Lismore shook his head, 'No . . .'

'Paddock somebody?'

'Nope, but we're getting there, keep them coming,' he added with a smile.

'Starter's orders?'

'Nope . . .'

'Furlong?'

Kenneth Lismore smiled, 'Furlong Freda. That's it.' He beamed. 'She had "Freda" tattooed on the back of her left hand and he called her "Furlong Freda". I don't know how she acquired the name but that was definitely how she was known. There will only be one "Furlong Freda" in York, I'll be bound.'

'It sounds like somebody we'll know, as you say,' Webster stood, 'most probably for petty stuff. Thank you, it's been helpful.'

'She acquired the name when she was a working girl; she used to work the racecourse.' Hennessey handed the file to Webster.

'Furlong Freda McQueen,' Webster read. 'Actually, just plain Queen, but calls herself McQueen. For some reason she changed her name between her last period of borstal training when she was nineteen and her first conviction for soliciting when she was twenty-two. She was a regular customer of ours until she was thirty-eight years old. She must have burnt out, as they all do, or got to be good at covering her tracks, but either way, we don't seem to have had a whiff of her for ten years, sir.'

'Time to pay a call on her, you and Ventnor, but it's been a long day, we can ease up.'

'We can, sir?'

'Yes, there will be no more victims. I didn't think there would be and the suspects I have in mind are not going anywhere.'

'I see, sir.'

'Dr Joseph at the university agrees, our suspects have "matured" as serial killers do . . . or as Furlong Freda seems to have done . . . they "burn out".'

Thomson Ventnor ate a ready-made meal that he had bought from the supermarket. Just one meal, which he carried home in a plastic bag; it was the only item he purchased and simply required reheating. After the meal he took a bus out of York to the semi-rural suburbs and to a large Victorian house set in neatly tended grounds. He observed swallows and swifts darting about in the summer evening air as he walked up the winding drive to the house. He opened the door and was met by a blast of heat which he always believed could not be healthy. He signed in the visitors' book and went up the wide, deeply carpeted staircase to a lounge area, where elderly men and women sat in high-backed armchairs, and where a television set stood in the corner. A young woman in a blue smock smiled at him. Ventnor walked across the floor to an elderly man whose face lit up with delight as he recognized Ventnor, but by the time that Ventnor had walked the few paces to where the man sat, the man had retreated into his own mind, so that all Ventnor could say was, 'Hello, Dad,' even though he knew he was speaking to a person who was little more than a vegetable.

Later, he returned to the city and walked the streets, and eventually fetched up in a pub he found to be pleasingly quiet. He bought a beer and stood at the bar. He thought of the issues . . . the transfer to Canada . . . the need to stay in York until his father had passed away . . . his passion for Marianne that did not seem to be diminishing.

It was Sunday, 21.45 hours.

SIX

Monday – 11.30 hours – 14.35 hours/Tuesday 16.50
hours – 17.30 hours
*in which a retired lady gives information and a decision
is made.*

'That's not the reason, darling.' Furlong Freda smiled
at the suggestion. She sat in a small chair in the
corner of the cluttered living room in her council
house in Chapel Fields. Outside, the garden was overgrown,
as were the gardens of many of the neighbouring houses.
The streets were lined with old, very old, motor cars.
Unpleasant odours lingered in the air as though a gas main
had been fractured, or a main drain had burst somewhere
beneath the road surface, and all exacerbated by the heat.
Freda Queen was dressed only in a tee shirt and shorts and
inhaled deeply on an inexpensive cigarette. The 'gaol house
tatt' described by Kenneth Lismore, 'Freda', was as he
described, prominent upon the back of her left hand. 'No,
they wouldn't allow working girls anywhere near the
racecourse, and the punters who go to the races are not the
sort of punters who are looking for a girl. A lot of them
have their wives and children with them. I mean, it's a
family day out, isn't it? And when the races are on the
working girls are sleeping, getting ready for night and the
trade in the night.' She inhaled and held the smoke in her
lungs before exhaling slowly through her nostrils. 'First fag
of the day,' she smiled, 'a lifesaver.' She flicked the ash
into the fire grate, which, like the fire grate in James Post's
house, had become a gathering place for any small
inflammable item. 'No . . . that stems from when I got lifted

for soliciting, years ago, darling, and the cop asked me why I was called "Furlong Freda", so I told him it was because I worked the racecourse, but I was put out at being arrested, that's why I said it, but the real reason is that I always gave value for money. I charged the same as the other girls but gave more . . . gave better . . . got a good reputation and had enough regulars not to have to take risks with strangers. I went the extra furlong . . . so I was "Furlong Freda McQueen". I called myself McQueen but my name is really just "Queen", plain old Freda Queen.'

'That we know,' Ventnor smiled.

'Never made no secret of it, darling.' Freda McQueen had a drawn, haggard-looking face and spoke with a harsh, rasping voice. She was in her fifties but could, thought both Ventnor and Webster, be taken for a woman in her seventies; Borstal training followed by a life on the streets does that to a woman.

From the room above came the sound of springs creaking, followed by footfall across the landing to the bathroom and the 'click' of the lock on the bathroom door.

'Punter?' Webster asked.

'Boyfriend,' Freda McQueen replied proudly. 'I'm retired, darling. I have boyfriends these days. They help me out financially but it's part of the relationship, not business. They don't hang around very long, just a few weeks at a time, but they're boyfriends.'

'I see.'

'So . . . Jim Post got iced did he? Little, no good, waste of space that he was. He won't be missed.'

'We hope you can help us?'

'Anyway I can, darlin', anyway I can.'

'You have a helpful attitude,' Webster smiled. 'You've changed your attitude to the police?'

'It was like this, love, I was what I was and the coppers who collared me was what they was, we was both of us just doing our jobs. It's the way the ball bounced in those days, dare say it still is, darling, dare say it still is.'

'Reckon it is,' Ventnor growled, 'and I reckon it always will be.'

'Oldest profession, darling, that's what they say and it's nothing about exploiting women. The game is the oldest two-way street in the world. The girls exploit the men just the same. Anyway the law helped me. I was being stalked and the cops put a stop to it . . . a real creepy guy, phoning me . . . the lot, so I called in at Micklegate Bar.'

'That's where we are based.'

'Yeah? Well they helped me; this is twenty, thirty years ago now. I didn't think they'd help a working girl but they did . . . sort of unofficial. The stalking stopped, just stopped. I found out later they . . . the police, had bundled this creepy guy into a car one rainy night and driven him ten miles out of York, dragged him into a field and gave him a slap, left him to walk home with a sore face and the suggestion that he worked a little bit on his attitude.'

Webster and Ventnor glanced at each other and raised their eyebrows.

'That wouldn't happen nowadays.' Ventnor turned his gaze back to Freda McQueen.

'It's the best way, if you ask me, it benefits everyone. I didn't get stalked no more, the police were not bogged down with paperwork and court appearances, and the felon avoided a criminal record. I've always said that a slap from a copper on a dark night up some snickelway is better than having to stand at the charge bar getting your record adding to, and your prints and DNA on file. I'd prefer a slap to a criminal record any day.'

'Which is why that sort of thing doesn't happen any more,' Ventnor explained. 'These days we like fingerprints and DNA on file. All right, it means paperwork but in the long run it makes our job a lot easier.'

'I can see how that can make sense.' Freda McQueen grappled for another cigarette and lit it with a flourish of a dull gold-plated lighter.

'So, you've retired from all that anyway?'

'Yes, old and past it and on the scrap heap with one or two boyfriends, like him upstairs,' she pointed to the ceiling just as the toilet was heard to flush, the bathroom door unlock and a heavy footfall return to the bedroom. 'He's stamping his feet because he doesn't like visitors, but it's not his house is it and he's not paying. Last Christmas Day my dinner was beans on toast. Well . . . it was just another day wasn't it, darling?'

'For some . . . sadly, it's like that.' Ventnor spoke with some finality. He wanted to get the interview back on track. 'So, James Post?'

'Yes . . . what about him?'

'What do you know about him?'

'Pretty well everything there is to know . . . and that isn't much . . . little man in every way. I tell you, even if they cremate him and put his ashes in an urn he'll occupy a bigger space than he ever carved out for himself in this world. We kept each other company and yes, we knew each other in the biblical sense, didn't mean anything to either of us. Then I realized just how low I had sunk when I woke up to the fact that I'd taken him for a partner. He lived at the bottom of the pit, right at the end of the line . . . five feet nothing of me . . . me . . . me . . . all about him and full of resentment, burning up with it and wanting victims, not just one, but more than one. It was then I thought I can't do this, I can do better, even I can do better. I didn't want to be seen with him. Who you are seen with is who you are, that's why I used to work in Hull and Leeds in the main.'

'We noticed from your arrest record.'

'Well, York's a small city; there are people I don't want to know what I was. A lot of girls go out of York to work for that reason.'

'Yes, so we believe.'

'Jim Post,' Ventnor growled. 'How did you meet him?'

Furlong Freda nodded to the television set in the far corner of the room, on top of which was a half-full bottle of vodka. 'I'm on top of it now.' She flicked the ash from her cigarette into the fire grate. 'Half a bottle between the two of us last night, just half a bottle, time was when I could sink two bottles a day by myself. Time was when that half-bottle would have been my breakfast. Time was, if it was booze it went down my neck. Never got as far as drinking brass polish but I was on my way there. I can't ... I don't want to think what my insides are like,' she shook her head vigorously. 'I carry a kidney donor card but when they lift my kidneys they'll take one look at them and then show them to medical students as an example of what an alcoholic's kidneys get to look like. Mind you, I suppose that is still some use, not the use I intended, but still use. Anyway, I woke up in the gutter once too often and thought that's it, AA for me, darling girl.'

'I thought you might say that,' Webster spoke softly. 'It's a theme in this inquiry.'

'About Jim Post?'

'That and a wider inquiry. So you went to AA?'

'Yes, and that's where we met. We helped each other get dry and then he introduced me to a couple he knew, and I joined their breakaway group.'

'Breakaway group?'

'Jim Post introduced me. He took me along one night to a cafe in York and I met this really nice couple, Ronald and Sylvia ... really charming. They just were able to make me feel good about myself. They said that they had been part of AA and got tired of it ... same old same old ... folk talking about how much they used to drink, and clearly exaggerating, and meeting the same people who were just addicts. Once addicted to booze they had become addicted to AA and lived just to attend the meetings. I was beginning to feel the same about AA. They got me off the booze ... but those meetings ... and Ronald explained that his group was just an alternative, but instead of listening to guest speaker's talk about their battle, we'd just sit in a cafe and chat, drinking coffee and killing the evening. So, I began to go along to that, met a few people.'

'Remember any names?'

'Helena and Roslyn . . . just two names . . . no surnames, sorry.'

'It's OK.'

'Once, twice a week, different people, men as well as women, but then I fell out with little Jimmy Post and never went again. I also found out that they were not friends with Jim Post, they used him, he was their gofer. I didn't want a boyfriend who was somebody's gofer.'

'I see.'

'But there was something going on. Jim used to have me photograph him in remote places.'

'How did you get there?'

'He was Ronald and Sylvia's gofer, he used their car. He'd got a driving licence when he was sober and never lost it. He just never drove; he never could afford a car, so never got done for drunken driving. So when he dried out he had a clean licence, very useful for someone who just runs errands.'

'All right, that explains something we wondered about.'

'Oh?'

'Yes, we have acquired some photographs showing Post standing in rural locations, sometimes he is looking at the ground. Someone had to have taken them or he used a timer device, or both.'

'Well probably both because I took some photographs of him. He was very insistent about the place, the place seemed more important than the photograph of himself somehow.'

'Can you remember any of the locations?'

'Just one with any certainty.'

'One out of how many?'

Freda McQueen shrugged, 'Twenty? He took me all over

the Vale from here to the coast, up into North Yorkshire and down into Lincolnshire.'

'We have some photographs of him but not that many.'

'He took a lot. He did his own developing.'

'Yes, we found his dark room.'

'He will have stashed his negatives somewhere,' she paused. 'You know he said something once. We were driving back in their Lord and Ladyship's car and he said, "This is my insurance" . . . or—'

'Insurance?'

'Or protection . . . he might have said protection. In fact I think he did say protection. Then he said, "If I go down, they come with me".'

'If I go down they come with me?' Webster repeated.

'Yes, word for word that's what he said. I asked him what he meant and he said "nothing" or "never mind" or something like that.'

'And you can only remember one of the twenty or so locations?'

'Yes, he seemed to know where he was going, didn't mess about, always took us right there. The booze had left some of his brain without damage.'

'Can you show us?'

'Yes,' Freda McQueen smiled, 'buy me a pub lunch and I'll show you exactly where.'

'You're on,' Ventnor replied. 'It's a deal.'

Freda McQueen stood. 'Just let me claw my kit on. I can't go out to a posh village dressed like this.'

Forty-five minutes later, Webster slowed to a stop in the car park of the Black Bull pub in the village of Temple Chitton, having followed Freda McQueen's directions. They stepped out of the car into fierce sunlight.

'See what I mean?' Freda McQueen announced, 'About this being a posh village?'

The two officers looked about them. Near at hand, the car park of the Black Bull contained Range Rovers, a

Bentley, two BMWs and a large, very large Mercedes. Further afield the houses of the village seemed to be mainly conjoined, each painted in bright blue and yellow pastel shades and each with a sound roof; clearly very well maintained properties. Further afield there stood larger houses in their own grounds, the land clearly marked by black painted metal railings or generously varnished wooden fencing.

'Yes,' Ventnor felt a bead of sweat run down his forehead, 'there's money here all right. How do you know about this village, Freda?'

'You mean, the likes of me should come here?' Freda McQueen grinned. 'You mean, I'm not posh enough, darling?'

She had changed into a long denim skirt with a red blouse and red shoes. Cheap clothing but she seemed to have done all she could to 'look her best'.

'I didn't mean that, Freda. I didn't know this village existed, it's off the beaten track but it shouts of money.'

'Old money, darling, they like to keep themselves to themselves. I know it because I used to visit the colonel here; he was one of my regulars. He lived in that house over there.' Freda McQueen pointed to a well-appointed cottage painted in brilliant white, with the wooden beam and doors and window frames painted in equally bright gloss black paint. 'He died some years ago.'

'You visited him here?' Webster could not hide his astonishment.

'Yes, during the day as well,' McQueen grinned then she tapped the side of her nose. 'Didn't dress like a working girl, see, though I was discreet. I dressed in a tracksuit and carried a bag. Arrived on the morning bus and actually did housework, washed down the door and the ground floor windows in me pinafore, walked to the shop for cleaning stuff and furniture polish, then went inside so no one thought anything else but that Mrs Mop was calling to "do" for the colonel . . . once a week. Then I left on the afternoon bus back to York, but that's why I remember this being one of the places that Jim Post took me to take a photo of him. He never knew that I knew this village and I never told him. He paid well. The colonel I mean, not Jim Post.'

'So where is the place Jim Post had you photograph him standing?'

'Not yet, darling, I'm hungry, I haven't had a proper meal for two days. Hope you have a lovely thick wallet; food doesn't come cheap in the Bull. Not cheap at all, darling. Once I've eaten, then I'll take you there, where he had me photograph him.'

The man smiled at the woman and softly spoke, 'It is time,' he said.

The woman returned the smile and replied, 'Yes, if you say so, then it is time.'

Dr D'Acre emerged from the heat of the white tent which had been erected in a corner of a field, some half a mile from the village of Temple Chitton, and brushed a fly from her face. 'Male,' she said, 'comparatively recent burial . . . some clothing still intact, but definitely male. Some flesh still in evidence but almost skeletal. Strange place to dig a shallow grave,' she glanced around her. 'Well tilled soil, not very remote. I would have thought someone would have noticed that some digging and burial had gone on . . . but . . . that's your neck of the woods Chief Inspector.'

'I was thinking much the same but that's for later discussion. Right now we have a deceased male in a shallow grave exactly where an informant said it would be.'

'You've got more than that.' Dr D'Acre smiled and allowed herself a brief and fleeting eye contact with Hennessey.

'Oh?'

'Yes . . . you've got a corpse with a present for you.'

'Really?'

'Yes, really, there's something in the mouth. It's a plastic bag. It could have been used for a gag, but it would be difficult to force into someone's mouth, and I can think of more convenient forms of gagging someone.'

'So can I.'

'So I felt it with my fingertips and there is something inside it . . . small and thin . . . difficult to tell what because of the layers of plastic, like a lump in a carpet which feels like it should be caused by a child's glass marble, but when you lift the carpet you find it's caused by something the size of a pea. So it's probably smaller than it feels to me but there is something in the mouth. I could take it out now but I'd prefer to do it in laboratory conditions.'

'Yes,' Hennessey spoke softly, 'I think that would be better especially since there might be other "presents" for us.'

'Good point. Will you be observing for the police?'

'Yes, definitely.' Hennessey also looked about him, the field of wheat, the small stands of woodland, the green rolling hills beyond and the ridge of skyline which gave to a clear blue sky. 'Yes,' he turned to Dr D'Acre, 'yes, I will definitely be attending this one.'

Nigel Post, pale of face, drawn of expression, opened the door of his house to Carmen Pharoah. 'Yes!' he said, with a mixture of curiosity and aggression borne out of a sense of being threatened.

'Police,' Carmen Pharoah showed him her identity.

'Yes?'

'About your brother . . . your late brother, James Post.'

'Yes?'

'My boss, Mr Hennessey, asked me to call and see you.'

'Mr Hennessey?' Short Nigel Post looked up at the statuesque Carmen Pharoah. 'He's the gentleman . . .'

'Yes, he was with you when you identified James Post.'

'Yes, nice man,' he glanced across the road and noticed curtains begin to twitch. 'You'd better come in, keep the nosies guessing.'

Carmen Pharoah read Nigel Post's house, neat, clean, cramped. All seemed appropriate to her for a man of Nigel Post's age and social standing. She accepted his invitation to sit. 'There has been a number of developments in respect of Mr James Post's murder.'

'Oh?' Nigel Post sank into an armchair opposite Carmen Pharoah.

'Yes. I am not at liberty to disclose anything, I'm afraid, not yet.'

'I understand, miss.'

Carmen Pharoah thought Nigel Post seemed lost. 'This can't be easy for you?'

'Well, first it was my wife, now it's my brother, both taken before their time. My wife was knocked down and killed by a drunken driver and now James. You can't help just sitting here and thinking about them when they were alive . . . what we did together . . . the conversations we had . . .'

'Yes, I do understand. Really I do.'

'You've lost someone?'

'Yes . . . yes, I have,' Carmen Pharoah remained stone-faced, 'but can we keep this relevant, it's about James.'

'Yes. Sorry.'

A fly appeared as if from nowhere and began to buzz noisily against the window pane. Nigel Post rose from his chair, opened a window and the fly found its escape route.

'Most men I know would have swatted it,' Carmen Pharoah commented.

Nigel Post resumed his seat. 'I prefer to feed the birds and spiders. So, how can I help you?'

'James took photographs.'

'Yes, he did.'

'We have found some but the indications are that there

are many, many more. So the question is, do you know any place that your brother might have placed any photographs or photographic negatives for safe keeping?'

'Old technology,' Nigel Post commented, 'so few folk talk about photographs and negatives, it's all digital cameras with lots of pixels . . . whatever a pixel is. But James did use a conventional camera so he dealt with negatives and prints.'

'Do you know where he might have kept them, somewhere other than his house on the Tang Hall Estate?'

'His "drum" he used to call it. There's only one place I can think of.'

'Oh?'

'His bank.'

'His bank?' Carmen Pharoah paused and then said, 'You mean within a safety deposit box?'

'Yes. It's a long shot but it's the only place I can think of.'

'They've paid off before. Do you know which branch of which bank?'

'Yes, I think I do. He wrote me a cheque once and I framed it,' he smiled and stood.

'You framed a cheque?'

'Yes, I'll explain when I come back down.' Nigel Post left the room and was heard by Carmen Pharoah to go upstairs and then return a few moments later. As he re-entered the room he handed Carmen Pharoah a small photograph frame in which was a cheque made payable to Nigel Post for fifteen pounds and dated some ten years earlier.

'It was only fifteen pounds I lost, and when he gave this cheque to me in repayment of a loan I sensed that it was probably the only thing I was going to have to remember him by. So rather than cash it, I framed it. Anyway, he did once mention a safety deposit box he had at that branch.'

Carmen Pharoah took her notepad and ballpoint from her handbag and copied down the bank's name and address and the number of James Post's account therein.

*   *   *

Dr D'Acre carefully removed the plastic bag from the mouth of the deceased and equally carefully began to unfold it. She found it stiff and brittle with age, but eventually she removed a credit card, which had expired some three years previously and the name on the card was one R. E. Malpass. She handed it to George Hennessey who took it in his latex gloved hands and read the name with some satisfaction.

'The net closes.' He smiled as he placed the card in a self-sealing cellophane sachet. 'The net closes.'

'That is your suspect, I take it?'

'One of them . . . it is a husband and wife duo.'

'You'll be arresting them?'

'Now we can. With this credit card they can be at least linked to this murder, but it is still less than we need to prove guilt . . . but it's a significant step in the right direction.'

'See what else I can let you have.' Dr D'Acre turned her attention to the body on the dissecting table, which was still clothed in the remnants of the garments he had worn when murdered. 'I think this post-mortem is going to be inconclusive, even before I start, unless there is a significant injury such as a skull fracture. I don't think I am going to be able to determine the cause of death . . . but a note of his clothing . . . odd shoes. I mean a different shoe on each foot, an old duffel coat, still discernible as such only one toggle out of the original three remains and look,' she gently pulled away a thin thread which appeared to have been wound round the waist of the deceased, 'this is the remnants of twine. So who wears odd shoes and ties his coat together with string?'

'A down-and-out.'

'Yes,' Dr D'Acre replied with a solemn tone, 'yet another person to be given a name and buried. I can determine stature and age at death to see if he matches any missing person reports. The credit card would put his burial at in excess of three years earlier than his remains were found . . . though there, I encroach on your territory.'

'Oh, please, as before, encroach all you like,' Hennessey replied, having retreated to the wall of the pathology laboratory as protocol dictated.

'Right, let's get the remains of the clothing off shall we, Eric?'

Eric Filey reverentially stepped forward and assisted Dr D'Acre with the slow removal and cutting away of the clothing, many pieces of which crumbled to the touch.

'Summer burial,' Dr D'Acre said calmly.

'Summer?' Hennessey repeated questioningly.

'I would think so, just a shirt and a vest under the duffel coat. A down-and-out would know where to obtain woollens, Salvation Army . . . institutions like that.'

'Yes . . . good point.'

'Easier to bury as well,' Dr D'Acre added. 'Easier to dig a shallow grave in summer time, the soil would be frozen in winter.'

'Indeed.'

'The trousers now, Eric,' Dr D'Acre announced. 'We'll cut them away, I think.'

Filey turned and took a large pair of scissors from the tray of instruments and then slowly and methodically began to cut the trousers from the bottoms to the waist, and, as he did so, Dr D'Acre probed gingerly into the pockets.

'Different socks also,' Dr D'Acre pointed to the feet of the deceased, 'one dark one and one white one. He really was a down-and-out. Hello . . .'

'You've seen something?' Hennessey took an involuntary pace forward.

'Probably . . . probably,' Dr D'Acre peeled the right-hand sock away from the partially decomposed remains of the lower leg. 'This sock seems to be . . . yes . . . something has been pushed down here.' She carefully extracted a plastic coin bag, Hennessey noted, of the type used in banks to contain a determined amount of the same type of coin. Dr D'Acre handed it to him and taking it from her he saw that it contained a piece of paper neatly folded up.

'I'll get this off to the forensic science lab at Wetherby. This will make interesting reading,' Hennessey murmured as he gingerly unfolded the sheet of paper. 'Well, well, it is a utility bill. Part of one. The part you keep . . . sent to one R.E. Malpass of Hutton Cranswick . . . and dated three years ago. Somebody is leaving us presents, indeed.'

'Indeed.' Dr D'Acre began a careful examination of the body. 'It looks like murder,' she said. 'The stomach has been punctured.'

'That's of significance,' Hennessey growled.

'Yes, someone didn't want the stomach gases to bloat and then burst the stomach. Usually it is done when a corpse is immersed in water to prevent it rising. A bloated corpse will rise and will even bring heavy weights to the surface with it, but if burying in a shallow grave it's a good idea . . . from the felon's point of view that is, it's a good idea to puncture the stomach to allow the gases to seep out because the stomach will expand and push away unconsolidated soil and then explode with such force that it could expose the grave. Someone did not want this old boy found, but who would want to go to such lengths to hide the body of a tramp?'

'Someone who enjoyed murdering as an end in itself,' Hennessey replied calmly. 'Someone who didn't want to be stopped until he had satisfied the need to take life.'

Dr D'Acre glanced at him. 'The name on the card?'

'Yes,' Hennessey nodded, 'the name on the card.'

'But how would a tramp obtain the credit card of the person who was going to murder him? How would a tramp even know the significance of a credit card?'

Hennessey shrugged. 'I don't know. Perhaps . . . perhaps . . . Malpass was taunting us. That is unlikely though, or perhaps a third person was leaving us a present, or perhaps a third person was maliciously implicating Malpass who is completely innocent. Perhaps, perhaps, perhaps . . .'

'No dental care to speak of, but that is in keeping with one of his lifestyle. No evident fractures, the skull appears to be uninjured, the skeleton is intact. Unless he died of natural causes, he was suffocated or strangled, and no evidence of same will have remained after being in the ground for in excess of ten years. As I said, an inconclusive post-mortem.'

'But helpful,' Hennessey held up the two sachets he held. 'It's going to be very helpful.'

The office was small, smaller than Carmen Pharoah expected it to be. It was neatly kept and clean, with no softenings that she could detect in her initial visual sweep of the room, no framed photographs or plants in pots, it was all very functional and to the point. The man behind the desk was well-built, and easily six feet tall, and thus seemed to make the room look even smaller,.

'Yes, I am aware of the safety deposit box, a yellow one, quite an unusual colour, and also quite the largest such box that can be obtained in the high street, strangely light as well, I have always thought.'

'Light?' Carmen Pharoah asked as a double-decker bus whirred past the building.

'In terms of weight,' the bank manager, 'Edward Edwards' by the nameplate on his desk, replied, 'very large and very light. So whatever is in there, it's not the family jewels or gold ingots. I am sorry to hear about the death of the customer; Mr Post, did you say? But I am afraid I can't release the safety deposit box in question without author- ization from his next-of-kin or a court order compelling me to do so.'

Carmen Pharoah smiled. She put her hand into her large leather handbag and extracted a manila envelope.

'I anticipated you,' she spoke triumphantly, 'signed by a judge in chambers less than an hour ago.'

It was Monday, 14.35 hours.

Tuesday, 16.50 hours

Hennessey, Yellich, Ventnor, Webster and Pharoah passed the photographs between them in a solemn silence. It was little wonder, as Carmen had said, that the large yellow safety deposit box was so light, it contained nothing but photographic negatives; hundreds of them, and most of the victims of Ronald and Sylvia Malpass, clearly taken discreetly by James Post, and one or two showing the Malpasses in circumstances which linked them to the murders.

'A very small camera without a flash attachment,' Webster murmured as he handed two of the photographs, which were still damp from the developing process, to Ventnor.

'Sorry?' Hennessey queried.

'Just a comment about the camera, sir,' Webster explained, 'the only way he could have taken these photographs was with a very small camera, small enough to conceal from Ronald Malpass, and one which would not flash when the shutter was pressed. He must have kept the aperture at its widest.'

'Yes, he was determined to take them, the Malpasses, with him if they silenced him or if he was arrested. I bet it was Post who slid the credit card into the mouth of the tramp, and pushed the utility bill into the tramp's sock ensuring it was preserved in the plastic coin bag. He told Furlong Freda that he had "insurance". I bet you that was what he meant.'

Hennessey paused. 'Still largely, if not wholly, circumstantial but this one,' he turned the photograph he was holding around and showed it to the team, 'this one I like muchly. Shows Ronald Malpass emerging from the kitchen garden . . . broad daylight; it indicates that they left the women in the kitchen garden at Bromyards in the "quiet period" in the morning, thus avoiding telltale headlights going to and from Bromyards in the dead of night, and if seen would have taken to be legitimate callers to the house and the elderly Mr Housecarl. It seems to have been taken from a distance of a couple of hundred yards away so Malpass would not have heard the shutter click. He was taking out insurance all right.'

'Very leisurely attitude,' Yellich added, 'calmly walking about and separating from each other by that sort of distance. It clearly wasn't a hurried job, no dashing up to the house, locking the victim to the chain and dashing away again, they hung around . . . very cool . . . very collected.'

'Yes, nonetheless, unless we find something in the Malpass's house it is still going to be an uphill struggle to secure a safe conviction but these photographs and particularly this one,' he tapped the photograph showing Ronald Malpass walking out of the kitchen garden at Bromyards, 'this one is enough to arrest them and have them remanded. Separate them; give them a taste of prison life. It depends on the quality of their marriage of course, but with luck, she might roll over on him when she sees this photograph. If she turns Queen's evidence, well, we'll see what we see. We'll get the warrants tomorrow morning and bring them in. There's no hurry, they are not going anywhere or about to murder someone else. They're washed up.'

It was Tuesday, 17.03 hours.

Wednesday 10.15 – 10.40 Hours

Sylvia Malpass, tall, elegant, even in the blue and white tracksuit she always wore when doing housework, stood patiently in the back room of her house in Hutton Cranswick and felt a strange and unexpected sense of calm and contentment. She smiled gently as she looked out of the wide window to the rear of her home, to the large well-tended garden, where her husband was, at that moment, playing water from the hosepipe over the shrubs and the lawn, and doing so despite the recent rain and looming rain clouds. Yet, he always did that, always watered the garden before leaving the house for any length of time. That day, though, Sylvia Malpass thought that she observed a certain determination, and certain restlessness, about her husband's actions. It was, she thought, as if the garden was parched, and baked dry and hard, after a prolonged drought. She pondered whether or not she should interfere . . . normally she would not do so . . . his was the garden, hers was the house, seemed to have been the unwritten rule which had evolved in their home-building, but the excess of water drenching the garden did, on this occasion, eventually reach her. There was also, she told herself, other things which had to be addressed. With that thinking, with that argument in her mind, she turned and walked to the kitchen and exited the house by the rear door. She walked calmly up to her husband, approaching from his left and side so that he had sufficient notice of her arrival. It did never do, she had learned early on in their marriage, to take him by surprise. His reaction in such circumstances could be at best dangerous, at worst deadly. He turned at her approach and welcomed her with a warm, very warm, smile.

'You've been doing this for well over an hour, darling.' She spoke softly, yet managed to project a note of protest.

'Yes . . . I know . . .' he replied equally softly, 'but it makes me feel better . . . and I always do this before we go away for a while . . . you know that.'

'Yes, darling . . . but . . . but . . . ' she pressed the heel of her sports shoe into the lawn causing a deep indentation. 'Look at that . . . what my heel has done . . . the garden is waterlogged . . . you are drowning the garden.'

'You can't drown a plant.' Malpass continued to spray the shrubbery. 'They have a kind of shut off valve which activates when they have had sufficient to drink . . . but I want the garden to be well-watered . . . I don't like fretting about the garden when I am away, or we are on holiday. It spoils everything for me.'

'Yes, darling . . . but even so . . . enough is enough, and there's other things to be done.'

'Perhaps, but I still have the front garden to water.'

'The front . . .' She rested her hand on his forearm. 'What will the neighbours think when they see you watering the garden in this sort of weather? It rained last night and just look at these rain clouds approaching.'

Ronald Malpass glanced to his right and saw mountainous grey clouds menacing in the east. 'No hosepipe ban yet . . . so why shouldn't a fella care for his plants . . . and since when have I been worried about the opinion of the neighbours?'

'But,' she protested, 'as I said . . . still things to do . . . we need to fill the car with petrol for one thing.'

'Oh . . . yes, all right . . .' He laid the hosepipe on the ground. 'Confess I had forgotten that . . .'

'Well, we won't get far on an empty tank.' She smiled.

'Certainly won't.'

'I'll make us some coffee . . . we both need a break.'

'Yes . . .' Ronald Malpass smiled at his wife. 'Yes,' he said again as their eyes met. 'Yes. Coffee. A coffee with you would be good. Very, very good . . . just once more before we set off.'

Sylvia Malpass returned to the house with a spring in her step; her husband by contrast, walked with a powerful determined heavy footfall across the sodden lawn to where the hose was attached to a tap set in the wall. He turned the tap off, screwing it down firmly, and then entered the house, wiping his feet on the mat as he did so.

Some moments later, Ronald and Sylvia Malpass sat in identical armchairs facing each other in a living room, which had been tidied to perfection, and the air in which was heavy with the smell of furniture polish and freshener.

They each sipped coffees from cups which, like the armchairs, were identical.

'It tastes exquisite,' Ronald Malpass commented. 'You know that I often say that the first cup of coffee in the morning is the most enjoyable cup of the whole day . . . the most enjoyable by far, but there is something refreshing about this cup of coffee. It is special somehow.'

'I know what you mean, darling. I thought that the garden had a certain freshness about its fragrance as I walked out there just now . . . something which I hadn't noticed before.'

'That is probably because I had watered it, doing that always releases the scents . . .'

'Yes, but even allowing for that . . . there was a definite something other . . . something now in the air.'

'Perhaps.' He sipped his coffee. 'Perhaps, but it's possible because it is often like that before you go on a journey . . . you seem to have a heightened sense of awareness of your surroundings. It's a bit like saying goodbye to a house just before you shut the door behind you for the last time.'

'My mother used to do that.' Sylvia Malpass looked upwards as if recollecting memories. 'I never have . . . I dare say I was always looking forward. My old dad, he used to say that she must be soft in the head to talk to empty houses, but he was a hard case. I take more after him than her . . . and I could never take to the other thing she always had us do – which was that before we left the house as a family, even if it was only for the day, we would sit and pause for a minute or two, and I mean just for sixty or one hundred and twenty seconds or some time in between, to collect ourselves as a family before going out. Even if there was a taxi waiting outside with the meter ticking, down we would sit . . . in silence . . . then we could leave the house as a family.'

Ronald Malpass pursed his lips. 'You know, I quite like that . . . and you never told me that . . . not in all these years . . .'

'I didn't, did I . . . I just remembered it now for some reason. Probably because you never did that, paused before leaving the house, and I never wanted to do it anyway. I just left it behind in my childhood along with the dolls and tea sets.'

'But as I said . . . I quite like the sound of it. I could quite take to the practice.'

'Well, we can do it today if you wish. Especially before this journey, when we don't know where we are going.'

'Yes . . . just getting away from here . . . away from Hutton Cranswick and the Vale of York altogether.'

'How long do you think we have got?'

'Time yet.'

'But they're coming?'

'Oh yes . . . yes . . . they're coming. So long as we are well away by then. That is the main thing.'

'Yes. It's all done upstairs. All neat and shipshape and Bristol fashion . . . just as my Master commanded.'

'My Master . . .' Malpass smiled and drank the last of his coffee. 'You haven't called me that for a long, long while.'

'My Master and Commander. I haven't, have I?'

'Yes, that was it . . . My Master and Commander.'

'I just stopped for some reason . . . I dare say that our marriage moved on as marriages tend to do . . . a continuously evolving process.'

'Dare say. . . . When did you first use it? Can you recall?'

'Oh . . . that would be in Ireland . . . I am sure it was during the Irish venture.'

'That was fun. You were like a coyote.'

'A coyote . . . a wild dog . . .' She raised her eyebrows. 'What on earth do you mean?'

'In the mid west of the USA, so I once read, the coyotes who live outside small towns send a bitch on heat into the town . . . and dogs just cannot resist a bitch on heat, and those dogs who are not tethered or kept in doors will form a pack and follow the coyote . . . these are domesticated dogs, people's pets, and the bitch leads the pack of pet dogs out of the town where the other pack, the coyotes, are waiting. Carnage.'

'Wow . . . I'd like to see that!'

'So would I . . . What I'd give to be a bird in a tree looking down on that.'

'Yes . . . not just the bloodletting, but the anguish of the pet owners . . . all that guilt for not keeping their family pet safe. But we . . . I didn't attract a pack, just one at a time. Remember we called it the Black Widow game.'

'Yes. That was it.'

'The one with the black wig, and into the bar . . . sitting alone . . . grief stricken young widow . . . just lost her husband . . . allowed myself to get chatted up, and eventually asked if he knew a place where we could go because I have my needs . . . but somewhere close . . . they all did and it was guaranteed to be isolated . . . and you followed us . . . dressed in black with a black painted pickaxe handle. You know that's where we learned the value of changing the MO.'

'Yes . . . once semi-conscious from the pickaxe handle, we did the business . . . one got drain cleaning fluid down his throat . . . we left him choking his life away . . . that was a bit noisy . . . we were isolated enough . . . but I was worried by the racket he made . . . learned the value of silence there.'

'Yes. The old learning curve was steep in those days.'

'Another had a plastic bag pulled over his head; the third had his throat cut; the fourth had a knife shoved into his chest . . . picked up after ourselves . . . left nothing behind . . . no prints . . . nothing, and the glass you drank from in the bar would have been well washed and dried by the time each body was found.'

'Four of them . . . Dublin, across to Galway, then back via Cork and Waterford . . . well, not those places but little towns just outside them.'

'Never pulled that stunt in the UK.'

'Didn't, did we . . . that's because we hit on the idea of targeting alcoholics . . . but . . . Ireland . . .' Malpass smiled at the memory. 'That was a pleasant little jaunt indeed. Most enjoyable. And that was a pleasant and enjoyable cup of coffee.'

'Thank you.'

'I'll go and fill up the car . . . check the oil.'

'And I'll wash up . . . leave everything just so.'

'Yes . . .' Ronald Malpass glanced at this watch. 'Time is perhaps beginning to press a little . . . we must not leave it too late to make good our departure.'

'No . . .'

'So I'll leave the front garden unwatered. Get straight off when I return.'

'After sitting in silence for a minute or two?'

'Yes.' He held eye contact with her and nodded slowly. 'Yes, we'll do that . . . we'll do that.'

Wednesday 10.50 hours

Hennessey and Yellich sat in Hennessey's office in silence. Yellich glanced casually out of the small window towards the city walls and at the extended group of tourists thereon, who were enjoying a brief respite from the rain and also a period of sunlight created by a gap in the unseasonal cloud cover. Yellich watched as the tourists walked, having stretched into a linear group, ambling, looking to their left and right, bedecked with cameras, unlike the locals, who walk the walls singly, often with an air of hurried determination, staring straight ahead. Beyond the walls, over the rooftops, Yellich saw the upper parts of the three square towers of the Minster gleaming in the unexpected sunlight, with the heads of the tourists clearly seen atop the southern tower, all safely hemmed in with suicide-proof wire netting, despite the fact that no one in the thousand year history of

the Minster has ever deliberately flung themselves from its
height to their death. But this, Yellich reflected, was the
early twenty-first century, and health and safety issues rule,
as does fear of litigation, and the two, he saw as being inter-
linked. Yellich often thought, when beset with cynicism,
that the issue was not so much the safety of the individual,
but the safety of the organization concerned from legal
action being raised against it. He turned his gaze to George
Hennessey. 'You're quiet, skipper,' he said, smiling.

'Yes, yes . . .' Hennessey replied, forcing a smile as he
was pulled back to the here and now from deep and distant
thoughts. 'I was worried . . . confess I still am . . .'

'Worried, boss? Why . . .?' Yellich leaned forward, resting
his elbows on his knees with his hands clasped together.
'We'll lift them . . . there's nowhere they can go . . . even if
they make a run for it they can't hide anywhere.'

'Yes, I know . . . I know . . . but it's not that . . . I don't
think they will even attempt to run . . . it's not that at all
. . . I am worried about the number of victims that they have
taken . . . the old tip of iceberg . . . there's always more than
we know . . .'

'Yes . . . for sure . . .'

'So, just as more people went into Cromwell Street in
Gloucester than have been determined, just as the Yorkshire
Ripper would likely have taken more victims that the thir-
teen he was prosecuted for, even if they were not all fatally
injured, and just as Hindley and Brady were in all possibility linked to the disappearance of other children who
went missing at the time, but outside the Greater Manchester
area . . . so they were not seen as relevant . . .'

'You think that's a possibility, sir?'

'Yes. Why not . . . they had transport . . . they could have
got up to Newcastle or Glasgow very easily . . . come to this
neck of the woods or through to Hull . . . down to Birmingham
. . . but children from those areas who disappeared were not
linked to them because at the time Greater Manchester Police

were not looking outside their administrative area . . . but now
we know serial killers roam far and wide.'

'See what you mean, boss.'

'It's not the tip of the iceberg in that I am sure we know
of the substantial number of the Malpass's victims . . . but
there's always one or two or three more . . . and that's one
or two or three victims who won't get justice . . . or one or
two or three families that won't get closure.'

'We still have to chat to them, boss . . . they might confess
to others.'

'Yes . . . yes.' Hennessey nodded. 'Good point . . . they
might tell us more than we already know. Might. I still
feel that we have to hope that one turns on the other . . .
but if they both go N.G., as my son would say, then the
CPS still has an uphill battle. Being photographed standing
over the grave of a victim, Hindley-like, is not proof of
murder – not in itself – and, yes, we have the other photographs, and, yes, we have witness statements, but a defence
counsel with fire in his belly could make a jury reluctant
to convict. In Scotland it could even invite a "not proven"
verdict.'

'Yes . . . I see your concern, sir.'

'When this case comes to court it will be the trial of
the most prolific pair of serial killers ever known in the
UK . . . but, like I said yesterday, unless one rolls over
on the other it's going to be a similar case to Regina
versus Allit . . . a case wherein the accumulation of
circumstantial evidence becomes sufficient to convict . . .
being the most difficult to prosecute and being the easiest
to defend. But as you say . . . we have still to chat with
them.'

The phone on Hennessey's desk warbled. He let it ring
twice before picking it up. 'Hennessey . . .' he said, then
fell silent as he listened. 'All right. Thank you. We'll be
there directly.' He glanced at Yellich. 'They're ready now
. . . vans . . . sergeant . . . four constables, scene of crime

officers . . . just requires you and me to make up the arrest squad.'

George Hennessey strode determinedly up the drive of the Malpass's home in Hutton Cranswick. Yellich strode equally determinedly behind him, and following Yellich was a uniformed sergeant and two male and two female constables. Hennessey struck the front door of the house thrice with his open palm and shouted, 'Police! Open the door.' He then rang the door bell continuously, insistently.

There was no reply. There was no sound, nor any form of response from within. Hennessey turned and noticed a youthful tee shirt wearing couple stop and stare at the activity from the other side of the street. Beyond the couple were neatly kept houses, and beyond that, flat fields leading to a flat skyline, all under a grey, short-lived, cloudy sky. He found a brief moment to concede that police activity of that nature was not an everyday occurrence in Hutton Cranswick. He turned to Yellich. 'Take a constable and go round the back, please.' He banged on the door again. There was still no response. Hennessey stepped back from the door and nodded to the constable holding the ram. 'Put it in,' he said quietly.

The police constable stepped forwards swinging the ram backwards as he did so, and when close to the door swung it forwards as close to the lock as he could manage, and succeeded in bursting the door open at the first attempt. He stepped back allowing Hennessey and the sergeant and the three remaining constables to enter the house. Hennessey leading the way shouted, 'Police . . . police!'

The interior of the house was still and quiet. The house was, he saw, neatly kept with just a gentle whiff of air freshener mingled with the soft odour of furniture polish.

'Right,' Hennessey turned to the constables, 'search the house . . . every cupboard . . . every loft space . . . everywhere a human body can be concealed . . . you know the drill.'

Then he walked from the hallway to the kitchen and unlocked the back door using the key that had been conveniently allowed to remain in the lock.

'Flown the coop, boss?' Yellich entered the house followed by the constable, youthful, fresh-faced, white shirt, dark blue trousers.

'No . . . no . . .' Hennessey turned and walked back towards the hallway, 'no, they're here somewhere . . . they will not be running. It's over for them; I know that they know that.' He paused. 'Find them and then search the house for the evidence we'll need to convict them . . .'

'House is empty, sir.' The sergeant descended the stairs. 'We're checking the loft now but it's clearly empty. We checked everywhere . . . under beds . . . cupboards . . . no one here . . . just us.'

'Outbuildings!' Hennessey snapped, 'Check the out-buildings.'

The sergeant turned and shouted to the constables. 'Down here . . . check the garden shed . . . and the garage.'

Hennessey and Yellich stepped out of the hallway and into the living room of the house to allow the uniformed officers to pass.

Hennessey turned to Yellich. 'They can't have gone . . . they can't have!'

Moments later . . . perhaps less than sixty seconds later, the sergeant returned in a solemn looking attitude and looked at Hennessey. 'We've found something, sir.' He turned and led Hennessey and Yellich to the garage which stood beside the house, separated from it by a narrow concrete path. The door to allow a person ingress and egress to the garage was open . . . a constable stood beside it . . . the other constables stood behind him on the path. The sergeant turned and said, 'In the garage, sirs.'

Hennessey and Yellich entered the garage and saw first the gleaming coffee coloured saloon car owned by the Malpasses, within which Ronald and Sylvia Malpass, sitting as if asleep, he in the driver's seat, and she beside him in the front passenger seat, and holding each other's hand. A hose led from the cars exhaust to the interior of the car via a partially open rear window.

'We checked for life, sir,' the sergeant informed. 'Both appear deceased . . . no pulse and their skin is clammy to the touch.'

'Thank you, sergeant,' Hennessey mumbled. 'Thank you.'

A silence descended upon the scene broken by Hennessey who said, 'You know, I feel cheated.'

'Cheated, sir?' Yellich replied.

'Yes . . . they won . . . they won. Neither of them could have survived gaol and they knew that . . . not after their lifestyle, and they would have also known that for them it would have been life without the possibility of parole. We'll never know how many victims they had . . . the nine women in the gardens at Bromyards plus the tramps they left buried . . . or exposed . . . all over the UK . . . those that we know about. We got involved in it when it was all over, when they had already decided to quit on their own terms and escape justice . . . even if the price they were prepared to pay was the loss of their own lives . . . but they escaped justice. So, yes, I feel cheated . . . and their victims also . . . they were cheated out of justice.'

The man lay in bed looking at the woman who stood naked at the window, and who, in turn, was watching the sun sink over the Cumbrian fells, causing the autumn trees to glow like shimmering golden orbs. He savoured her slenderness, the soft curve of her breasts and the well-toned muscles, caused, he knew, by her passion for equestrianism. 'I should have known better.' He lay back and looked up at the ornate plasterwork of the ceiling painted in pale blue to blend with the slightly darker blue of the wallpaper, which blended with the yet darker blue of the carpet.

'You couldn't have done anything else,' the woman

half-turned and smiled at him. 'You had to wait until you had sufficient to justify an arrest warrant.'

'I still think I could have moved earlier, I just didn't think I was under time pressure once Dr Joseph told me she also felt they had stopped killing. I thought I had all the time in the world . . . and they won . . . they played the game they had planned to play and we'll never know for how many years they played it.'

'Or how many victims.'

'Yes, just silently took victims that few, if anybody, would miss and buried them locally, or left them to be discovered in remote places all over the UK, leaving local forces to do the naming and burying number, and not one was linked with another.'

'There was no reason why they should be linked, down-and-outs are always being found where they died . . . even in the twenty-first century, that is just the way of it.' She stretched her arms, 'This sun feels good. It'll be getting quite chilly outside, but behind the window, warmth comes through.'

'Yes . . . then, like all serial killers, they racked up the game and took victims who'd be missed. It was probably their way of bringing an end to it all . . . then we called on them.'

'By which they knew it would only be a matter of time before you closed down on them you mean?'

'Yes, that's exactly what I do mean,' the man levered himself out of bed, 'so they killed their gofer and then sat in their car in the garage with the engine running, holding hands as they drifted into their final sleep. Dare say they won in a sense, did what they intended to do without ever seeing the inside of a police station, let alone a prison.'

'Well,' the woman smiled at the man, 'all you can do is chalk it up to experience. Let's dress, I'm getting hungry.'

'Agreed.' Hennessey stood, reaching for a towel as he walked towards the bathroom. 'Something in the bar, then we'll eat. I think I'll try the duck myself tonight . . . confess it looked to be quite good.'

Louise D'Acre turned to take one last look at the setting sun, 'It was,' she said warmly. 'It was very good indeed.'